George Midgett's War

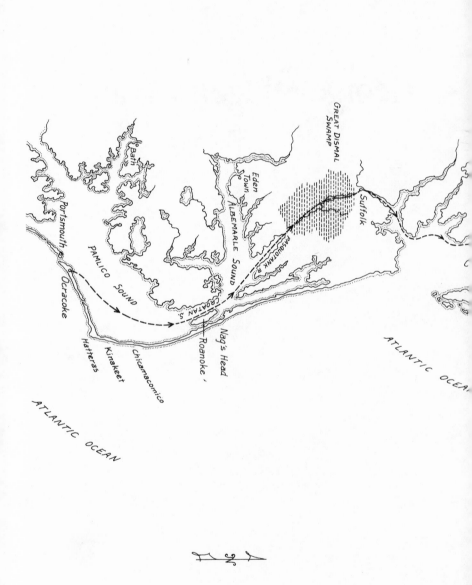

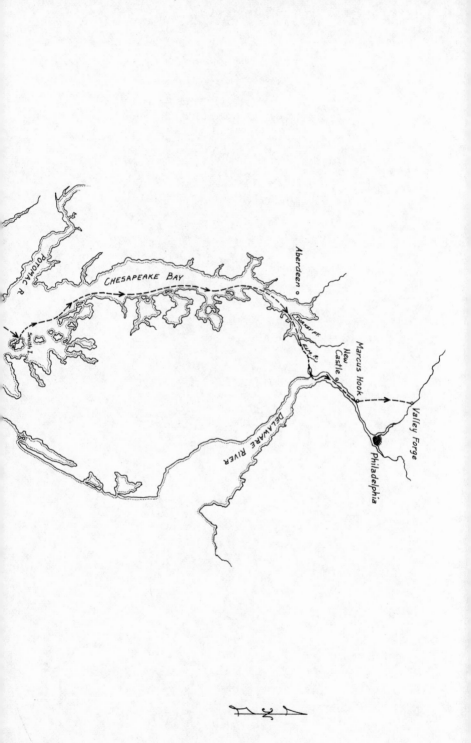

George Midgett's War

SALLY EDWARDS

CHARLES SCRIBNER'S SONS | NEW YORK

For Melba Long

Map by Jackie Aher

Copyright © 1985 Sally Edwards

Library of Congress Cataloging in Publication Data
Edwards, Sally.   George Midgett's war.
Summary: The residents of an island on North
Carolina's Outer Banks are unconcerned about the war
for independence until an incident causes a fourteen-
year-old and his father to set out for Valley Forge with
supplies for Washington's army.
[1. United States—History—Revolution, 1775-1783—
Fiction.   2. Outer Banks (N.C.)—Fiction]   I. Title.
PZ7.E265Ge   1985   [Fic]   85-1954
ISBN 0-684-18315-3

1 3 5 7 9 11 13 15 17 19   F/C   20 18 16 14 12 10 8 6 4 2
Printed in the United States of America

1

He was drowning again, lost in the rise and fall of a stormy sea. He awoke in the cold dark, nightmare-tense and sweating. He waited helplessly for morngloam, for daylight. Wind and sand scratched and hissed against his window. He could feel sand in his bed.

No house in the village of Ocracoke was chinked absolutely tight against blowing sand. Even here, in Erskin Midgett's house, sand was a part of every loaf of bread, every cup of tea, and Sunday pudding. People on the continent said there was so much sand in the islanders' stomachs it had become a part of their character. So much sand, ingested daily, made them queer. Not only queer, it was said, but wild and ungovernable.

George Midgett pushed himself elbow high and wiped the window clear with the warm palm of his hand. He looked out to the November-cold, gray day. The wind was blowing a topknot plume of brown mist off the sand hill just beyond his window. Sometimes a winter wind buried an entire forest of scrub oak or cedar in brown sand the color and texture of Barbados sugar. Thinking about sugar and the dark, sticky sweetness of Barbadian molasses made his mouth water.

He stared now, wide awake, at the sand hill, one of the many large dunes that protected the village from the Atlantic Sea, that more believably belonged somewhere else—in Africa perhaps, in a faraway desert he had seen in a picture book. It was no wonder that strangers, survivors coming out of shipwreck fever, at last summoning the energy to be curious, asked where they were.

Henry Frampton, the scholar bound for Bath Town, had looked out this same window and thought he had died. George had nursed Frampton for days, holding his thrashing arms quiet, forcing hot soup between his bruised and swollen lips, when suddenly Frampton opened his eyes.

"I'm dead," Frampton moaned.

"No, easy."

"I never was a good Anglican. I am dead and in Purgatory. Oh, God, have mercy on Thy poorest lamb."

"No. Only a broken leg, sir, and a fever and bad bruises. Easy."

Frampton raised his head and winced from the pain in his leg. "Alive! Who the devil are you?"

"George Midgett, sir. Erskin Midgett, my father, brought you ashore."

"To where? Where the devil am I?"

"Ocracoke Village, sir, on the Outer Banks of North Carolina, very near Portsmouth Island. Your ship was bound for Portsmouth and Bath. Don't move that leg."

"Shipwrecked! Ah, yes, I remember. I would be. Even appointed to the King's Academy in Bristol, I was always late for beginning of term. What day is it?"

"November twelfth, sir. You have been in fever for over a month. You are lucky, sir. You remember your name and your past life. Some survivors forget everything."

Frampton fell silent, thinking. "I see. Yes. Ocracoke, you say. Where is that?"

The boy took a spoon from the sick tray and traced a map on the quilt.

"The Outer Banks of North Carolina, between Portsmouth, Virginia, and Portsmouth Island, North Carolina. The Outer Banks start here, from the line of the Virginia Commonwealth—sand islands, barrier reef islands—running 175 miles from Virginia to Currituck Banks and Bodie Island and Chicamacomico and Kinnakeet and Hatteras to here, Ocracoke Village and Pilot Town and Ocracoke Inlet, and across the inlet to Portsmouth Island and Portsmouth Town. Over here, on the continent, is Bath Town, your destination. Up here, to the right of the continent, is Roanoke Island, where the Raleigh colony was lost two hundred years ago. Here, separating us from the continent, is Pamlico Sound. When you're able to travel, you can take a pilot boat from Ocracoke across the sound to Bath."

Frampton scowled. "Doubtless you have helped other strangers get their bearings. The cartographers in Liverpool should be so skilled. The continent, you say. Why, that's America. That's North Carolina. The continent? Why call it so?"

"It's so far away. Nobody ever goes there. We only go

3

down to Portsmouth. Everyone on Ocracoke calls it the continent. They think us queer in Bath. They call us yaupon eaters, because we make tea from yaupon holly. They say our skins are scaly, from eating so many fish and crabs. They say we have broad tails and thorny fins growing from our backs and webbed feet that keep us from wearing shoes."

Frampton laughed. "Why, surely you're an English citizen, the same as I am. You're an American colonist, the same as I hope to be. A cattymount, are you, a scaly-skinned freak? I see only a comely lad. Your name again?"

"Midgett, sir."

Frampton lay back on his pillow and closed his eyes. "I am not dead. I am not in Hell. Yet I am attended by an ordinary-looking boy whom others call a monster and who calls himself a dwarf. Midget, you say. You are indeed determined to be different."

"The Midgett name is an old joke, sir."

"I should hope so."

"Long ago a man washed up on Bodie Island, near Roanoke Inlet. It is said that he was so tall and so strong that the islanders called him a midget, and he took the joke as his new name, since he wanted to start a new life. He was Isaac Midgett. He was over seven feet tall and once carried a six-hundred pound ox through a swamp. The ox was stuck in a bog and Isaac Midgett lifted it on his shoulders and carried it free and—"

"Please." Frampton raised a frail hand. "Don't elaborate further. A joke. Doubtless everyone laughed. But wait . . ." he hesitated. "I have heard the name before. I am a scholar,

4

you see, and collect bits and pieces of source material." He reached for paper and pen and scribbled different spellings. "Midget. Midgett. Midgette. Midyett. Midyette. Miget. *Miget*. Ah, yes. That's it. From the French. That may have been the true name of your Isaac Midgett. He may have been a Frenchman, may have descended from a long line of ghosts, ghosts dimming back to medieval France, to the Holy Crusades, even to God's greatest angel, the Archangel Michael. St. Michael was 'Miget' to his friends, a nickname that means 'he who is like God.' Eh, lad, are you like God?"

"Why, no, sir." George drew back, startled.

"Never mind. A theory only. At any rate, Master Midgett, I am greatly obliged to you."

"Not to me, sir. To my father."

"I am his debtor. Did he by chance also save my luggage? I traveled with a chest of books. A scholar needs books like an old tart her memories."

"There was no value salvage from the wreck, sir, no furniture or plate." The boy reached for three torn, water-damaged books on a table and placed them on the quilt. "Only these scraps. Mind your leg."

"My English grammar. The picture book of Shakespeare. Plutarch's *Lives*." Frampton touched each book with care. "You call these scraps?"

"Books are not value salvage."

"No value? I'll want a word with your schoolmaster."

"We have no school here."

"Your parson then."

"We have a church, but no parson. If the weather's fair,

5

and if we can raise the money to pay him, a parson comes from Portsmouth."

Frampton scowled. "I take it that no one can read in this paradisial place."

"We learn the catechism. We sing hymns. We meet in church every Sunday, parson or no parson."

"Then my obligation to your father is paid," Frampton said promptly. "While my leg heals, I shall teach you your basic letters and how to write that celebrated name." He smiled. "The stories in these 'scraps' may prove that it is conceit enough to belong to the family of man, rather than a band of angels."

Frampton's leg healed much too soon. George remembered being nine years old and waving good-bye to the pilot boat, holding the gift of the three books in his arms. Frampton promised to come back for a visit, but he had never returned. As Burrus Wahab said, "Jonah never went back to the whale."

George turned from the window to the meager library in the bookshelf he had made himself. Shipwreck wind, so generous with other luxuries, was stingy with books. Books were too fragile to run the gauntlet of a storm sea. But he usually bought one book a year, on the annual trip to Portsmouth with his father and John Farrow. They would be going soon, before real winter set in and before the killing of the first pig. He put his mind off Portsmouth and then on the taste of the fine, fat pigs he had helped Hannah O'Neal raise. He was wide awake now. There was no sweat on his face, and his hands were warm and dry.

He heard the noise of his father beginning the day—bellows blowing new flame from ashes banked in the hearth, the thunk of a fresh log thrown on the fire, the thump of his father's feet squaring into his boots, the clink of spoon against mug. Hastily, as though physical action would erase the nightmare completely, he pulled a wool sweater over his wool shirt, jerked on wool pants, and hurried into the front room. His boots and socks were lined up on the cool end of the hearth. Jenny Scarborough was knitting new socks for his Christmas present, and he and his father would buy new boots in Portsmouth. Although he had cut gashes in his old boots, they pinched tighter every day.

Erskin Midgett gave him a mug of hot yaupon tea. He stood at the hearth, a tall, big-boned man with blue-green eyes, mostly green, dark red hair, and a red stubble beard. His eyes never twinkled, but there was warmth, even affection, in his calm, very direct gaze. His skin was as tough as whiteleather, the leather used in harnesses for draft animals, and no amount of bear grease, even if he had used it, would smoothe the calluses on his hands. He was thirty-five years old, but he had never looked young, nor would he ever look old. He lived against the wind, and the wind had scarred him ageless. Even in repose his body seemed to strain against an invisible force. He did not stand to his full height. Only when he was angry did the familiar crouch snap tall and intimidating.

"Good morning, son," Erskin said to George. "I have heard the news that Ballance Meekins will marry in the spring. I want you to think about his place in Farrow's boat."

George gulped the tea too fast and burned his tongue. He tore a piece of bread from the loaf on the hearth and stuffed it in his mouth. So Ballance Meekins would marry in the spring. Ballance was fifteen, only a year older than George. He would marry some poor unsuspecting lark from Chicamacomico. A good thing, George supposed, that some families still followed the tradition of pairing their children at birth.

Ballance Meekins had been in John Farrow's boat for two years. With his marriage, he was entitled either to his own boat or to a place in the lead boat, captained by Erskin Midgett. Whatever his choice, he would leave an empty oar in John Farrow's boat. There was always an empty oar in somebody's boat. In Ocracoke Village, just as in any village from Currituck to Cape Fear, the opportunity for a place in a boat was as certain as sunrise.

"What about old Hannah?" George asked. "If I go out with Farrow, who will help her with the pigs?"

Hannah O'Neal, deaf and mute as a result of shipwreck fever, had once lived with Erskin and George. Erskin had rescued her from the sea the year George was born. George didn't remember his mother, when she had died or when Erskin and Hannah O'Neal had moved from Kinnakeet to Ocracoke. He did remember when Hannah moved to a farm two miles north of the village. She raised pigs on the farm and supplied the islanders with winter pork.

When George's nightmare of drowning was new, when he had first screamed out in the night, Erskin never mentioned a place in a boat for George. When he was ten years

8

old, George began to help Hannah with the pigs. He collected leftover rations from the women in the village and carried them up to the farm in big buckets. He also cleaned the pig trough and strawed the pen.

"That is woman's work," Erskin said now. "This year you are fourteen. It is time you pulled an oar." Thinking deeply to himself, Erskin stared into the bright fire. It was when Erskin was silent that he spoke the loudest.

So his father had future plans for him. George laced his boots with fingers turned to thumbs. How could he ever take a place in a boat?

"I doubt any woman could carry those buckets so far," George protested. "Hannah is old and feeble. She'll always need a farmhand."

Erskin looked at his son with a broad smile. "Why, George, Hannah O'Neal could carry those buckets to the moon and back. So could Jenny Scarborough. Hannah will get on very well without you." He again turned back to the fire. "It was Hannah's own decision to live alone on the farm. She never mixed well. She only went out to Sunday service.

"When a Hatteras Indian put his farm up for sale, the last Indian farm to be sold on Ocracoke, we decided—all the men in the village—to buy it for Hannah. You should have seen the stock she started with—shoats no bigger than chickens. It was the village common consent to keep her house repaired and her larder stocked in exchange for pork. It was also common consent to provide the curing salt every year. Hannah figures her service to the community to the last tuppence, and vice versa."

9

"Then why was I sent to help her?" George stood up. "Nobody else has the stomach for what I do. I guess that's why."

"You were never sent anywhere," Erskin replied. "Hannah wouldn't be helped. She'd allow no one to lift a hand for her. If the slops for the pigs were put out in the village at morngloam, Hannah was waiting on the stoops in the dark. Not even Mary Farrow could reason with her." He paused. "We forgot that Hannah O'Neal is a survivor."

George understood. The survivors of shipwreck horror stood apart—the Hannah O'Neals, the Burrus Wahabs, the Jenny Scarboroughs. The eternal wind had not birthed them. The everlasting sand had not nurtured them. They had belonged elsewhere, to the out-there world, to softer, easier lands. Only satanic happenstance or divine predestination had brought them here, washed them up clinging to the last raw kernel of life itself. Survival had changed them forever. They had walked through the valley of death and come out distant and formal, the ordeal stripping their minds and hearts of all but the barest essentials. No survivor ever complained of hunger or thirst, of heat or cold, of too little or too much, or too late or too soon.

"But why me?" George asked, bewildered. "Why did you send me to the farm?"

"I told you you were never sent," Erskine repeated. "You were simply accepted. You remember the morning Hannah came by and you emptied our scraps into her bucket, and then you reached out and pulled the bucket out of her hand and followed her home. The next day you carried both buckets, and the day after Hannah didn't come to the village at all. Helping her was your own idea, and you were allowed. Hannah suffered you. As I recollect, you were very proud of yourself. Never say you were forced into unseemly work or that Hannah O'Neal is old and feeble. Say instead you're a boy no longer."

Erskin turned to George with firm decision. "When the blues stop running, we'll kill the first pig. When the pork is cured, you'll take the oar in Farrow's boat. The curing salt worries me in these troubled times. The salt is safe?"

Two 100-pound barrels of salt were buried in Hannah's cellar, salt worth its weight in gold in Portsmouth Town. Even in normal times, salt and sugar were the top commodities on the barter exchange. By common consent the previous summer, the villagers had bought an extra barrel of salt to last them two winters. At that time the British blockade around Ocracoke Bar and Portsmouth Harbor was having little or no effect. The large sloops and brigantines, some equipped with eight swivel guns, could not navigate the shallows of the bar or second-guess the shifting sand glaciers at the entrance to Pamlico Sound. At that time the British fleet of heavy warships was no more dangerous than a fat, half-asleep cat watching a thousand mouseholes.

But there was big money to be made by running contraband through the weak blockade. If high-level policy in London dictated that rebellious American port cities be cut off and starved by blockade, the policy also paid handsome dividends to runaway slaves and pirates. They provided skillful, safe passage for captains of neutral ships into Portsmouth Harbor—for large bribes. These sea highwaymen

11

grew greedier and demanded more money. Sharp merchants in Portsmouth passed on the hidden blockade tax to their customers. Prices doubled, then tripled, then quadrupled between the summer and fall of 1777. Anything and everything could be bought in Portsmouth, at the cost of higher and higher inflation.

The salt in Hannah O'Neal's cellar caused worry because it grew more valuable every day. Everyone in Ocracoke knew where it was hidden, including Austin Etheridge, the richest man in the village, who owned warehouses and a town house in Portsmouth. Etheridge had lately voiced the opinion that there were better uses for the salt than curing pork. Purchased for 80 guineas a barrel, it could be resold for 200 guineas—with a substantial profit for every villager and a handsome brokerage fee for Etheridge.

George watched his father's frown deepen. "Aye, it is safe," he said. "I checked the cellar yesterday. When we go to Portsmouth, we should ask about the war. If it goes on much longer, maybe we should put a guard on the salt."

"War?" Erskin chuckled. "You mean Burrus Wahab's war? The old man spends mornings with his spyglass, watching the British fleet. He has been charting the blockade pattern for a year now, warning against rape and plunder. It gives him something to talk about in the public house—a harmless pastime for a poor fool who lost his toes in the blubber room of a whaler, then was washed up here. But, son, put no faith in Wahab's war. In truth, there is always war on the continent. Indian wars. French and Spanish wars. Now a civil war between Englishmen. But it is not our business. We fly no flag here on Ocracoke."

"A raiding party hit Kinnakeet last week," George said. "Two cows were slaughtered and their carcasses left on the beach. That was no rumor."

Erskin scowled faintly. "Aye, they were raided, but they used those cows as bait, hoping to capture a British longboat and hold the sailors for ransom. It is a sorry, old-fashioned trick, brought over from the Irish islands. Who would believe, in this day and age, that any candle flicker seen ashore would fool a smart captain? That trick no longer works. The Kinnakeeters hang lanterns around horses' or cows' necks and expect an English captain—the best captains in the world and most of them Irish—to steer clear of the light and sail straight into ambush waters. No wonder they lose their cattle."

George knew the trick had worked hundreds of times, even for men of Ocracoke. But he doubted that British longboats had been lured ashore by lanterns. Burrus Wahab had told him that if Kinnakeet cattle were slaughtered, it was because the small, isolated village had no defense against raiders.

"There is no war here," Erskin repeated. "Etheridge trades with the British captains. Business as usual. We'll use one barrel of salt for curing and bring the other to the church for safekeeping."

"I'll see Hannah through the winter," George said slowly. "I'll think on the other."

13

"You'll waste little time thinking. No Midgett man, none I ever knew, refuses the sea."

Erskin was suddenly gone, the fall of the front-door latch echoing in the room. For a long moment George listened to the wind. "No Midgett man ever refuses the sea." The fire no longer warmed him and the tea and bread sat in his stomach like stones.

2

He started at the dock end of the village and worked his way along the crescent line of cottages. They were two- and four-room turreted houses, built of pine and oak logs mortared together with sand and oyster shells. Pine and scrub oak were plentiful on Ocracoke, but the best timber came from wrecked ships. Seasoned teak and mahoe, Jamaican mahogany and South American birch. Nameplates from wrecked ships identified the houses. Burrus and Mollie Wahab lived in *The Monkey Foot*, the Farrow family in the *Geoffrey S. Cairns*, the Ballance Meekins family in *Ralegh's Swallow*. The greatest trophy—*The Polly Blue*—belonged to Erskin Midgett, but he had sent it to Portsmouth, along with the wreckage, to decorate *The Polly Blue* Tavern.

The houses were set on stilt bases, allowing storm water to wash through from the ocean to the sound. The stilts were nearly always buried in sand. Only a gale wind could sweep the village clean and add a second-story dimension to houses that now looked like a row of Puritan heads in church: the turret tops like gray caps set on gray, two-window-eyed faces buried in folds of brown sand.

Weathered, windswept, protected only by the sand-dune barrier, the houses, like the people inside, were fragile toys in the hands of the sea. The islanders might disparage a gale by calling it a "breeze," but such a breeze could flatten a house in seconds. A hurricane gale, or "strong breeze," could create an inside vacuum so quickly that a house simply exploded.

But the angry force that could tear the earth asunder could also bestow consolation prizes of great value. The sea had given the people of Ocracoke everything they had. Timber for their houses, linens for their beds, any number of household appointments that touched their rough, wind-tortured lives with elegance—all was largesse from the sea.

Inside the houses, a connoisseur's eye would have recognized treasures. Oriental rugs, their violent, faraway colors muted by submersion in salt water; pewter mugs and silver goblets; silver knives and forks and spoons; rosewood chests; chairs carved in teak and ebony; gold barber-surgeons' kits; gold watches, hanging vertically from gold chains on the mantels, ticking loudly and chiming the half-hours like a ship's bell; leather traveling cases, equipped with pint and quart bottles of medicinal rum, brandy, and rye whiskey; even the two brass-studded buckets that George carried to Hannah's farm—all these mismatched but genuinely beautiful things would have been valuable elsewhere.

To George and everyone else, they were commonplace. Who cared if the new Farrow baby was teething on a snuffbox that had once belonged to a French nobleman? Everyone had rugs from Cathay and too many silver goblets. What everyone wanted now was pork roasts and chops, fine white sugar for Christmas cakes and cookies, and a holiday measure of Barbadian molasses.

As he emptied the leftover bread and corn gruel, fish and rabbit bones into the buckets, George noticed that the rations were growing smaller. It was the villagers' way of saying that it was time to kill the first pig. Now the nights were very cold. The November moon was full.

He stopped at the last house on the main path, Jenny Scarborough's house. Jenny, a widow, lived alone with her 13-year-old daughter, Grizelle. George set the buckets on the stoop and blew on his hands. Swiftly moving clouds blocked out the earlier bright sun.

Jenny baked bread for Erskin and George. She wove their shirts, knitted and darned their socks, and came to the Midgett house once a week to change linen and make sure wharf rats hadn't taken over the pantry. Erskin kept her supplied with fresh fish and whale oil. George kept her woodbox full. Both Erskin and George kept her roof leakproof with tar and crushed rock.

George rarely stopped anywhere except Jenny's house. She usually offered him a sweet. Although he had never known his real mother, he did not consider Jenny a substitute. Jenny would never kick a dog or let a cat starve, yet a certain aloofness warned people that they could come so far, but no further. She had a mean mouth when vexed. Like lightning, the meanness did not strike often, but you remembered it. George found Jenny Scarborough intriguing because his father loved her. He could not explain how he knew this. It was simply a fact he had always known, yet never understood.

Hearing his knock, Jenny called him inside. He gulped warm air. Jenny was winding wool at her spinning wheel. The weasel, a small, oblong board that was hinged to the wheel pedal, popped the correct measure. Jenny removed the skein of soft sheep's wool, patted it smooth, and hung it on a wooden peg on the wall behind her.

"I hate winding wool. Only when you begin to weave can you see what you're making. . . . I've nothing for the pigs today, but there's spice cake in the cupboard. Help yourself. We're having service this Sunday, and I drew the lot to make the parson's cake. Doubtless he'll preach against luxury. The women know I have sugar saved and no husband to bake for. So it was my lot to bake the cake—for a withered parson who preaches against sin where there's no chance for sin. Help yourself. I do my part, but in my own way. Mollie Wahab will wail a complaint because the cake's cut."

George cut a thick slice, savoring both the rare delicacy and the conspiracy. He saw that Grizelle was not at home. Grizelle was never at home.

"Then I'll have to fetch Hannah for service," George said. "I'll have to walk to the farm on Sunday."

"It would be nice if you did." Jenny nodded. "One more square added to the quilt of your character. It is the season to think of others and to show Hannah we care about her." Jenny fixed a new tangle of wool on her wheel and began to pedal quickly. "Besides, she has the pigs. She has two barrels of salt."

Grizelle was conspicuously absent at the exact time of George's visit every day. He no longer asked where she was. He was tired of being told that she was helping Mary Farrow with the new baby or studying the catechism with Mollie Wahab.

"It is time to kill the first pig," Jenny said. "You can tell Erskin I said so."

"The blues are still running," George said, "the blues and drum. He won't kill the first pig until the fleet draws empty nets." He wondered why his father and Jenny relayed messages to each other through him.

"The pigs will be old sows before Erskin stirs himself, else Hannah will be raided. A raiding party hit Kinnakeet and slaughtered eight cows. Left the carcasses on the beach to rot."

"Two cows," George corrected. "It was two cows, Jenny."

Jenny's eyes darkened. "Well, suppose it's two pigs here. Two pigs will feed a family for the winter."

"The British won't come here," George said. "Not with Austin Etheridge's trade and the guard at Pilot Town. My father says they won't raid Ocracoke."

"Your father," Jenny scoffed gaily. "I have no ears for what Erskin says. And what guard? The last guard that patrolled Ocracoke Inlet soaked themselves in so much rum they had to be quartered in the Bath prison house. Governor Caswell sent us a group of rabble who did nothing but drink and dance naked until dawn. Worse than the Corees or

19

Matchapungas. So much for the protection of the continent. Why should the British buy beef or pork when stealing is free? The British do what they please. I suspect they are just as tired of bluefish and drum as I am. They want fresh meat, just as I do." Jenny stopped her wheel and pushed at her hair.

When she was a girl, Jenny's friends had tried to do something with her hair. It was very fine, long, and straight. After Moncie Scarborough's death, Jenny had pulled it into a tight bun behind her neck. When she was nervous or angry, she pushed at stray wisps.

"I'll tell my father," George said quietly.

Jenny stood up and walked to the window. "I would tell him myself if I had breath to waste. Erskin's war is out there. All his joy and love is in the war out there. The sea will kill us all, certainly men like Erskin, who pretend to have no fear of it. The sea, the wind, the cold, and the dark, and now British ships sailing round and round like witches dancing a kettle to boil. Erskin says the kettle won't boil. Erskin leans against the wind and rules the world." She turned to George with a thin, lonely smile. "There is talk you'll take the oar in Farrow's boat. You'd be fool enough to take it."

George swallowed, hard. "Not fool enough, Jenny. Just old enough. I am fourteen."

"I had forgotten you were so old. Too old for nightmares then, and screaming fits, and throwing up when asked to hold a line. The last time you took a place in a boat, you almost killed Burrus Wahab."

George looked at his boots, his heart filling with rage.

Three years before, he had gone out with Burrus Wahab in a small dinghy. Burrus wasn't physically able to handle even a small boat, but the old man was restless, the day was calm and clear, and Erskin's lead boat stayed within a 600-yard range. Burrus, trailing a line off the stern, had somehow hooked a marlin. He yelled to Erskin, bound the line around his waist and asked George to hold it. Burrus couldn't land the fish himself. Erskin came alongside and fixed his harpoon when the fish, in a violent last spasm, hit the dinghy and split it in two. George dropped the line. Burrus couldn't swim. George couldn't swim. He had fainted. When he came to, gagging on his own vomit, he was lying in his father's boat.

"Never again," Burrus spluttered. "I'll not have the lad in a boat with me."

Erskin had never mentioned the incident again. Nor had Burrus Wahab. Such an incident did not have to be mentioned. The unspoken curse in every Outer Banks village was, "The man is strong enough, and brave enough, but I'd not want him in a boat with me."

"He wasn't killed," George said. "It was a long time ago, Jenny. Three years."

"You don't know what a long time is."

Jenny walked toward George and kicked away a small, oblong rug that lay between them. The rug covered a dark bloodstain. George had seen the stain before, but only the edges, only the mysterious hint of where Moncie Scarborough had died. It was a large stain. Jenny usually took great care to keep the rug exactly in place, but now she kicked it aside.

"*There* is a long time," Jenny said. "Ten years. Ten years I've tried to scrub this floor clean. Ten years of scrubbing with salt and lye. And nothing will take blood off a pine floor."

George looked up to the mantel, to a small, oval silver frame, to a portrait of Moncie and Jenny Scarborough on their wedding day. But it was so faded, so water-damaged, that only Jenny could see it.

Jenny's voice came from faraway. "You had nightmares as a child. You were always drowning. You talked in your sleep. You were lost in a storm and drowning. I sat with you some nights, when I couldn't sleep. When Hannah O'Neal went away, up to the farm, Erskin didn't want you coddled. But I would hear you crying, and my Grizelle was a good sleeper, and I would walk across some nights and sit with you. I know what it's like—being lost in a storm. I know how real nightmares can be."

"I don't have nightmares anymore," George lied.

"I am glad to hear it." Jenny looked at him, again with the thin smile. "It is the blessing of childhood to outgrow things quickly: colic and the nightly visitation of demons. Oh, I am glad to hear it."

She walked to the mantel, touching the portrait with her dark eyes. Suddenly she was lost in a tight, strange mood, looking into the small, oval frame as though it were a mirror, reflecting other mirrors, and those mirrors reflecting so much illusion they produced reality.

"You would not know my life, George Midgett. You would not believe it. You would never know that I was once young

22

and carefree, born in Down Hatherly, England, near the border of Wales. I was Jenny Bourne, the oldest of eleven brothers and sisters. My father was a farmer, left a field of rocks by his own father. We would sit in church, my family and I, and see ladies and gentlemen, tradesmen, doctors, and solicitors. And my father was born down, and he stayed down. I had a dream, even then. My father heeled into his born place without a murmur of discontent. I dreamed of a man who would not heel into his born place.

"I had an uncle with a shop in Bristol, a boutique for fine ladies. When he died, I was allowed to go to Bristol to help my aunt as a seamstress. Bristol is a young sister to London. I can still see the shining cobblestones and the tall houses and hear the wharf noise and smell the Bristol sea, foul and dirty when the wind was still, and see the ships riding at anchor. Girls my age, nice girls from proper families, weren't allowed on the docks. But of course we went there—to watch the sailors and the trading. I saw the trading with my own eyes. One cargo of indigo or sea island cotton from North America would bring a million guineas. Men would shake hands on the Bristol docks for a million guineas. The slavers were the richest men. The slave ships put out from Bristol to West Africa, to Dakar and Accabee, and the slave pens on the Gold Coast. The slavers were all churchmen, but worse than pirates, worse than pirates who sold their swords to France. Ah, yes, the slavers were the richest men.

"I met Moncie Scarborough in my aunt's shop. He bought a length of Brussels lace for his mother in North Scotland. I knew he was a sailor. I would never have married a sailor.

23

No sane woman marries the sea. But he had black hair and blue eyes and he courted me with soft words. The sea was only his chance to go to America. He wasn't a seaman. It was only a way to earn money. He had friends who had gone to America before, to Philadelphia, and there was a job waiting, an ironmonger's job, when he could save the money to get there.

"I didn't marry him until he had the money saved and the letter from Philadelphia guaranteeing the job. I was fifteen and Moncie was eighteen when we married. We were married four months when we went to the docks, but now as passengers, with tickets paid for and a new life waiting.

"We laughed, Moncie and I, walking the deck and holding hands. It would be different in Philadelphia, where an ironmonger made good wages and could look any man in the eye. I would have a garden, fruits and vegetables. No Bristol shopgirl had a garden. And I would have a husband working up to his own business and children growing up to whatever they wanted to be.

"It was a fine trip they had," Jenny said quietly, "that ignorant bride and groom, watching a bright Orion in the sky and dreaming Philadelphia.

"Until the storm hit. We sighted land and were moving there on a glass sea, when a squall sucked our ship into a tunnel of blackness. Two days we were lost in wind and rain, two days of begging God's mercy and some prayers being answered with the mercy of dying. At last we grounded here, on Ocracoke Bar. I remember horses on the beach and longboats in the surf and the screaming. Aye, screaming, since five ships cracked and shattered in that storm, and ours was the only one grounded close enough for rescue.

"Brave men saved us. I would never deny it. Bravery and foolishness. I knew it soon enough—the foolishness. But I didn't know, that night, my life would be so expensive. I didn't know it would cost me my Moncie."

Jenny now touched the portrait with her hand. "We were saved—Moncie, I, and the child in my belly. But we couldn't move on until Grizelle was born. By then Moncie had built this cage of a house. Then I was too sick to travel. Then it was winter and no pilot boat would hazard a trip to the continent. Then it was spring and summer, and somewhere Philadelphia vanished from the face of the earth.

"We never spoke of Philadelphia. Because Moncie was the captain of the lead boat. My Moncie was what your father is now. Erskin was up to Kinnakeet and Moncie was the leader of Ocracoke.

"I never married Moncie to tame or change him. I loved him. I would have married him anyway. I didn't need his promise. Maybe he didn't know himself. Maybe it was the storm, and the wind turning his life upside down, and the hand of God protecting his wife and unborn child. I don't know. But once we were here, lost in this Godforsaken wilderness, Moncie changed.

"People change, but only, I think, to what they were meant to be. I never spoke of Philadelphia. What was the use? The sea was his true wife, the other half of him.

"He said he owed a debt for our lives. He said he had made a vow and would keep that vow. I lived in terror of the cry, 'Ship ashore!,' because I watched his pride grow into a cancer. Moncie led the rescue boats. He had to be first, to push the first boat out, to rein the lines to the horses, to challenge the cold dark. Pride made him first. And foolishness."

She looked at George. "I pity a fool."

Then her voice rose in a sarcastic whine. "Ship ashore! The men of Ocracoke will drop a coffin when they hear that cry. They are not husbands or fathers when a distress cry sounds on the wind. When strangers call them to glory, their own wives and children are forfeit."

Jenny moved, and her shadow made the bloodstain darker.

"You have to go out, they say. But you don't have to come back."

"Someone went out for you," George said. "It is the law here. You have to go out. You don't have to come back."

"Oh, Moncie came back. They brought him home to me ten years ago last night. They laid him on the floor and he bled to death in my arms. No one was saved that night. No lamb was saved. He nearly choked to death on his bloody pride."

Slowly, tenderly, Jenny's foot pushed the rug back into place. "And *there* is a long time." She pushed at her hair, moved back to her stool, and pedaled the wheel.

"And there is the place in Farrow's boat. And you are fourteen. I pray you will be fifteen and sixteen. But your father gives you no choice. You will die out there. I fear you will die out there. It is hard enough to be born to it. You were not born to the sea."

George stood up and pulled on his coat.

"The service on Sunday," Jenny said. "Don't forget to tell Hannah."

"Back then," George said, "back in Bristol, you must have been a pretty girl."

"No," Jenny said. "I was never pretty, but I had spark."

3

He kept to the lee side of the sand dune that guarded the northern end of the village. The pumice-stone wind stung and scraped his face. His steady gait turned into a trudge as the dunes grew smaller. As a child, he liked to sand slide down the smaller dunes. He would climb to the top, clasp his knees together, lower his head, and let the wind push and spin him, a human ball, down the slope. The shock of stopping would send him sprawling, legs and arms flailing, and then he would lie, tired and happy, spitting out sand.

But he could not carry garbage buckets, heavy even when empty, and sand slide. The dunes grew higher and the wind grew stronger, and he had burdens above and beyond the buckets. He knew exactly when the view would open up and reveal the sea. Hannah O'Neal's farm was surrounded on three sides by the sea. He knew when he was almost there.

He had not fooled Jenny Scarborough. It was impossible to lie to Jenny. But the nightmares weren't so bad. He slept until morning now, and if his legs were locked tight and he dripped with sweat, at least he had not wakened and cried out in the night. He had not disturbed his father. He had not disturbed himself. He was always drowning, of course, and lost in the dark, and although he never quite drowned, neither was he rescued. But it was not so bad now. He slept until morning.

He wondered if Ballance Meekins had ever been afraid of anything. Ballance Meekins would marry in the spring.

He wondered if Grizelle Scarborough ever thought about him, ever actually cared about him. Grizelle would go away to the female academy at Bath in the spring, her skin smooth with buttermilk care and her eyes bright with her mother's plans for her.

By dint of his own cowardice, he would be the pig boy still, going out once more to tend Hannah's new shoats. The only change would be that the wind would be blistering hot instead of stinging cold. He would turn his back on the sea, as no Midgett man had done before. He hated the sea, was afraid of it, was terrified and destroyed by the thought of it. He saw it now, wild and angry and cold and gray, venting full November force on the bleak, brown beach. He would not go out there. He simply would not go.

He would talk to Hannah O'Neal about it. He did not remember when he had first started talking to Hannah. In the past four years, they had had so much time together. When he was there, doing his chores, Hannah was always near, watching him.

One lost, long ago day, he had begun to talk to her. About how Burrus Wahab had lost his toes. How Austin Etheridge gave short measure to the merchants in Portsmouth. About Mary Farrow's hard time having the new baby, such a hard time that an axe was brought into the birthing room to cut the pain. About his father and Jenny. His father had too much pride to ask her to marry him. Nor would Jenny marry the sea a second time. They hardly spoke to each other at church or when they met on the main path. And that was how everybody knew there was love between them.

He told Hannah that reading was very difficult, and writing even more so. He would never have understood Shakespeare without the pictures. But his writing was improving. He was learning to keep his hand relaxed, and his loops were more graceful.

Hannah O'Neal, who could not hear, listened with her eyes. He talked out of his own loneliness. He knew that somehow she heard.

Today he would tell her about the place in Farrow's boat. He would tell her how sorely afraid he was. If she thought him a coward, she could not tell him so.

He looked up to the slate sky, filled with flowing mare's tails. Snow was in the sky. Looking ahead, he saw the outline of Hannah's fence. The buckets weighed heavier and he trudged faster.

The gate to the pigpen stood open. It was not unusual for the gate to stand open. Hannah often let the pigs roam free, knowing they would return when they saw George filling the trough.

But the gate was not open in the right way. He moved faster, running, struggling to keep the buckets balanced. The gate had been torn open. The top wooden slats hung loosely from the hinges. The pigs were nowhere to be seen. There had been seven pigs the day before, and three shoats.

He put the buckets down. He stood absolutely still.

Hannah was lying in the mud just inside the gate. As usual, she was dressed in black wool, but the black shawl that covered her hair was cast aside. George knelt and touched the soft, white hair.

Her eyes were closed. Her mouth was set in a firm line of triumph, almost a smile. A faint line of brown mud ran from her left cheek to her neck.

He wrapped the shawl around Hannah's head and shoulders. He could not see the blood on the black wool bodice, but he felt it. He lifted his wet hand. Stunned, he sat back on his heels. Then he saw Hannah's right hand, closed in a fist. He pried the fingers open.

A brass button, torn from a blue worsted fabric, lay in the center of Hannah's fist. One brass button.

He put the button in his coat pocket. His throat felt swollen. He lifted the body carefully, turned it slowly, and inspected the wound closely. He wiped his hand clean on his pants. Hannah O'Neal had been stabbed to death.

4

Jenny Scarborough and Mary Farrow shrouded Hannah's body, wrapped the frail, black-clad figure in heavy folds of homespun. Erskin and George dug her grave. The first winter storm, blowing shards of ice off waves cresting higher and higher, cancelled the arrival of the parson from Portsmouth. But Hannah O'Neal was accorded every respect.

A determined hermit, a human island cast adrift on a desolate island, at last she joined the community. Everyone in Ocracoke attended the funeral. The youngest mourner was the new Farrow baby. The oldest was Burrus Wahab. The sad proceedings reminded Burrus that he would soon pay his own debt to nature. Thus he stood upright, unmindful of his feet, and turned his craggy face away from the open grave to the wind. Grizelle Scarborough, recently acquainted with the Bible, recited the Twenty-third Psalm. The villagers, led by Erskin, offered the Lord's Prayer. Then, one by one, they picked up handfuls of freezing dirt and bade Hannah a personal good-bye.

"You were one of us," Mary Farrow said.

Erskin Midgett bowed his head but did not say anything.

"I had a mind to know you better," Burrus Wahab said. "I had a mind once to take you some cider. Wish't I had."

"Godspeed," John Farrow said.

George Midgett bowed his head but did not say anything.

Jenny Scarborough, pushing at her hair, looked long and hard at the small, narrow mound. "I wouldn't spit on a British sailor if his guts were on fire."

"May God keep thee in His bosom forever," Mollie Wahab said.

When everyone had passed by, the people, newly aware of the life and warmth that flowed between them, huddled together and departed. Only Erskin and George stayed behind. Erskin pulled off his frock coat, picked up a shovel, and began to complete the burial. For a long moment George was unable to help his father. The salvage chests of fine clothes, stored away and covered with mildew, had been opened. George thought only that he had never seen his father in black trousers and matching frock coat. Nor Burrus Wahab. Nor John Farrow. The men of Ocracoke had looked like Portsmouth gentlemen for Hannah O'Neal. The women, too, had adorned themselves with Easter splendor. Mollie Wahab wore white kid gloves. Jenny Scarborough wore the small filigree brooch she wore only at Christmas. Mary Farrow, lacking any jewelry save her wedding ring, wore her silver thimble on the thimble finger of her right hand. George had polished his boots with bear grease and borrowed one of

Erskin's black ties. Now he felt near to choking. He untied the tie, unbuttoned the top of his shirt and knelt to pack the dirt on Hannah's grave firm and neat.

Tears rolled down Erskin Midgett's face. He made no effort to hide or brush them away. George turned aside. He was not embarrassed to see his father cry. He knew there was no sorrow in his father's tears, only a black anger that seemed to deepen. George had never seen his father so troubled. Inside turmoil had rendered Erskin near speechless since Hannah's murder. Not once, not since George had hurried to the village to tell the mournful news, had Erskin expressed an opinion as to what had happened. Now he did, in a voice oddly flat and alien.

"A strange fate for a strange woman, to be stabbed by a British bayonet, trying to protect her pigs. It always hurt Hannah to have them killed. Of a summer night, I've seen her with an apronful of corn, feeding the shoats, making sure each one got his share. When Farrow and I went up with the knives and tubs, she went inside and drew the curtains. She never took her share of pork. Turkey and venison, but never pork.

"It was a large raiding party to take ten pigs. Three longboats for certain, with four oarsmen in each boat. Last year, even six months ago, the British would never have come ashore without pilots. Now they use longboats with great confidence. I wonder at that. I wonder at the bribe that bought such treachery—to tell them where to go and how to get there.

"I wonder at Hannah's mettle. Why did she leave the

34

house? The moon or morngloam gave light enough. Nothing wrong with her eyes. She could see the danger. Yet she went out. She pulled a button off her murderer's coat, even as her life leaked into the mud."

"They didn't have to kill her," George said. "Hannah couldn't have stopped them. They could have had the pigs without killing her."

"Aye." Erskin stared at something George could not see. He spoke quietly. "Even with the wind, and the roar of yonder sea, there is nothing so quiet as a new grave."

Erskin stuck the shovel in the dirt and suddenly straightened to his full height. "Aye, the British tars wanted fresh meat, but there was more purpose to the raid than to steal pigs."

"What other purpose?" George asked.

"Intimidation. Fear is a hard weapon. The wise general first sounds his trumpets to make his enemy afraid, then shows his steel. But the war on the continent means nothing to us. We've no quarrel with England. Far from it. Every man on Ocracoke has traded with the British, and Austin Etheridge has made a new fortune on the blockade."

Erskin pulled on his frock coat. He reached in a pocket for the brass button. "Why do the British provoke us now? Men so clever and cruel they made an old woman sport. One man, I surmise. Ordinary seamen don't wear blue worsted with engraved buttons. An officer killed Hannah." He turned the button in his hand. "Each village makes its own law. The Kinnakeeters were beaten at their own game. We shall not follow their example."

"There's the cannon at Pilot Town," George said.

Erskin almost smiled. "Blackbeard himself couldn't blow that cannon. It was spiked years ago by salt and sand. Besides, David doesn't always kill Goliath. The British now ride longboats into shallow inlets and cays. To burn our village, our homes and church, would be a short night's work." He paused. "I wonder. The careless thief often leaves the greatest treasure behind. The salt, lad." There was new anxiety in the question Erskin had asked only the day before. "When Farrow and I fetched the body down, you stayed behind to lock Hannah's house. Did you check the cellar?"

"Aye. The salt is worth more than twenty pigs."

"Only now we have no pork to cure."

"But Jenny says we can sell the salt and buy fresh meat in Portsmouth—"

"She voted to buy only one barrel," Erskin interrupted. "She said hoarding so much salt for so few people would bring down the wrath of a storm." He fell silent and scuffed at the ground with an angry, restless foot. "But, aye, it is valuable and all the more troublesome."

"A salt machine," George blurted out without knowing why. "When John Farrow last went to Portsmouth, he bought Mary a sturgeon roe. He gave me the newspaper the roe was wrapped in. The army on the continent has no salt. Salt is now more precious than laudanum. One of the Patriot radicals in Philadelphia is offering a reward of fifty guineas to any person who can find a method for taking salt out of the sea. His name is Franklin, Benjamin Franklin. He pleads for the invention of a salt machine."

"Two barrels is hardly a machine."

"It's two hundred pounds. It is enough to last the village for two years."

Erskin looked at him carefully. "I wonder. Now it will spice greed that needs no spice." He held out the button. "Keep this. It is Hannah's last gift to you."

Erskin did not go to the public house for his rum and pipe that afternoon. Instead, he hung his gold watch back on the mantel, took off his good suit, and put on his fishing pants and a sealskin jacket. He took his long knife from his tackle box, the knife that had once killed a tiger shark, and stuck it in the top of his boots. Then he asked George for the key to Hannah's house.

George, watchful and quiet, remembered when Erskin had killed the shark. It was when he had first known that his father was different from the other men. The shark had lured and trapped a porpoise in the shallows of Ocracoke Beach. Natural enemies, they fought to the death. The fight lasted for hours, the shark darting for the porpoise's underbelly with rattlesnake accuracy, the porpoise butting him aside. The shark had speed, but the porpoise had a stubborn, battering-ram nose. At last the porpoise beached the shark and arced, blowhole snuffling, to safety. But the beached shark would not die. It lay in a terrible spasm, with its head crushed and helpless fins flapping. The villagers enjoyed the spectacle of the dying shark. All except Erskin.

He came on the scene in late afternoon, after docking his boat. He ran forward, taking his long knife from his boot, straddled the shark, pulled its head back and slit its throat.

Then he lifted the shark and hurled it into the crowd. "Eat it," he commanded. "I would to God you choke on your amusement."

"A deserted farmhouse is fair game," Erskin said. "I don't worry about the neighboring Indians. Croatans and Algonquins are also our good friends. But shadows move in the night, and all are suspect in these times. Keep the fire. I'll bring the salt down. Tomorrow we'll take it to the church and each man will be assigned watch duty."

George heard his father taking the dray cart from the lean-to behind the house. The sound of the cart was soon lost in the wind pulling the sea to high tide. George thought idly that the sound of the wind, of sand scratching, sand popping and beating against windows, had never troubled Hannah O'Neal. But Hannah had kept her fire, both without and within.

George wondered why she had done it. He wondered if the officer, brass buttons gleaming in the half darkness, had been surprised. Would he have killed her if she had surrendered easily, feigning drooling, trembling senility? An officer was a leader, an example. Would an officer, George wondered, have committed murder without cause? Would he have shamed himself before his men with the murder of an old woman? Surely Hannah had done something unforgivable. Perhaps she had simply stood there, her dumb tongue thundering defiance, and humiliated the officer beyond control. Perhaps a woman who could not talk had spoken so loudly she had to be killed.

George did not take the button out of his pocket, but he

could feel it burning there. The button warmed his faint courage. He imagined himself coming over the last sand hill in the nick of time, hurling himself forward to protect Hannah, first flinging garbage swill into the brass-buttoned, blue worsted face, then using the buckets themselves to drive them all, all of the king's men, away. Then he would have soothed Hannah, assured her that he was not hurt and had not been afraid.

He stirred the fire and moved to the far side of the hearth. As his face cooled, so did the hot dreams in his mind. He had not been there. No one had been there. Only Hannah O'Neal knew the truth, and the truth was buried with her now-freezing flesh.

Wind blowing under the house chilled his feet and legs. His head, bereft of dream, throbbed with hunger. He was tired of potatoes and jerky, of tough, dried meat that tasted like mule meat. He was tired of drum and bluefish. He could taste a Christmas ham, richly glazed with honey and cloves.

Nor was his hunger merely physical. A demon question mark danced behind his closed eyes. For now he had no choice. The long way to Hannah's farm—the chance to hold his head at least halfway up—was closed. The small approval he had earned from the villagers for his service—"But four miles up and back, George, don't you get hot? . . . But four miles up and back, George, don't you get cold?"— would no longer be forthcoming. Even Jenny Scarborough's mockery could not change the fact that the only road now open to him led straight to the sea.

His head throbbed and his heart ached. Years ago, it

seemed, Hannah was being murdered as he wakened from a nightmare. Hannah lay lifeless in the mud as he hastened forward to tell her that he was afraid. And now he could hear the ghosts, the multitude of Midgett ghosts, who laughed and beckoned to him.

"Where is he? He's never here when most he's needed."

Startled, George looked up. He had not heard Jenny come in. The filigree brooch at her neck shone as brightly as a star against her black cape and the darkness in her face.

"To Hannah's. He went to fetch the salt."

"There is mutiny in the public house. Every man clamors for his own wisdom and strategy. Etheridge, of course, says the murder was an accident, an unthinking mistake. We are to go on as though it never happened. Old Burrus would take on the British fleet barefisted. Farrow sits brooding over ale gone flat and sour. Only your father can decide. The men are on the way now to tell him so."

"How did you get into the public house?" George asked, amazed.

"Why, I walked in, the same as any trousered fool. What man notices a woman when it's up to him to save the world? Why, no. Can a man's mind hear a woman's heart? I pulled my own glass of *anejo* and sat at Erskin's empty table." Jenny pushed at her hair and walked to the fire and poked it savagely. "Mollie Wahab and Mary Farrow sit at home sobbing and praying. They pray for angels to come and deliver them. I expect no such favors. I will save myself and my child. We'll go to the continent, if necessary."

"Not in this weather," George said. "No pilot boat can take you to Bath until spring."

Jenny quieted. "I have been in weather before. Get out your father's traveling case, and mind his p's and q's."

George set out Erskin's traveling case of pint and quart bottles of rum and brandy. He was placing glasses on the table when the knock came, and Jenny opened the door.

Only three men came—Austin Etheridge, the native son who had made good in Portsmouth, Burrus Wahab, and John Farrow. The late afternoon wind had not cooled their tempers on the way from the public house. Etheridge's normally pale, counting-house face was as red as a moon rising over a storm sea. Burrus' weatherbeaten complexion was dead white. Only Farrow resembled his usual self. Farrow, in fact, gave George a wink as he poured his glass.

"Take wide berth, lad," Farrow said softly, "and may you be the father of your children." He drained his glass.

"He went for the salt, the barrels of salt in Hannah's cellar." George addressed Etheridge. "He'll be back soon."

"Ah, then. We'll wait." Etheridge poured himself a large tumbler of brandy and eased into Erskin's chair. "Now, see here, Wahab, Erskin is a practical man. When the occasion demands, he is a man of soft answer and turning the other cheek. In my opinion, this occasion so demands."

"You are a sniveling ass," Burrus rasped, limping forward for a glass of rum. "You would compromise your own village. Erskin Midgett is an eye-for-an-eye man, and so am I. You, at least, won't be murdered in your bed. You can sit safely in your town house in Portsmouth and wait for news of our massacre."

"Easy, sir. I am a man of Ocracoke and proud to be so. I seek only the best interest for all concerned. Certainly none of us espouse the foolish notion of separation from England. None of us can rightfully be accused of Patriot sympathies. But we are colonists—"

"Don't tell me what I am," Burrus rasped, "nor what I espouse. You and your big words. I damn them. Actually, I am a lapsed Unitarian out of Nantucket Island, but it is not up to you to tell me what I am."

"You are a sitting duck," Etheridge retorted. "Like it or not, you are in the cross fire of a war. Like it or not, in wartime, when civilians are in the wrong place at the wrong time, they get hurt."

Burrus took a long swallow, then pulled out his handkerchief. "I am not hurt. No Ocracoke family is hurt. Only Hannah O'Neal—"

"Oh, come now," Etheridge said impatiently. "She was a poor old hag living on borrowed time. You didn't know she was alive, except at pig-killing time."

"We know she's dead," John Farrow said quietly. He looked at George and Jenny, sitting together on the hearth. "It is different now, Etheridge."

"How so? The village has lost ten pigs. What more is there to steal? Accept the loss. Stifle the noise of revenge and go on as before. Think of your women and children."

John Farrow spoke without anger. "Is that what it means

to you—that we have lost ten pigs?" Slowly, he finished his glass, stood up, stuck his hands in his back pockets, and began to pace the room. "They always happened somewhere else—the raids. Up to Kinnakeet or Chicamacomico. Other people, always other people, lost their cattle—their lambs and sheep and cows. But I never heard of murder. We knew but pretended all was rumor or gossip. Still, I never heard of murder." He stopped in front of Etheridge. "Surely it is different, Austin, now it has happened here. Surely it is more than ten pigs."

At last Etheridge lowered his head. His three chins spilled over his high, stiff collar. Burrus Wahab blew his nose. John Farrow returned to his chair.

"We lost the pigs," George heard himself saying, "but there is the salt."

"Aye," Jenny echoed. "The salt."

Etheridge recovered instantly. "Aye, and I was coming to that at the proper time. I have been telling you for months that you could sell the salt for eight times the original price. I could act as your broker."

"A mess of pottage!" Burrus fairly exploded. "You would trade a woman's blood for how much? What is your portage fee after your brokerage fee after your—"

The front door swung open. Erskin stood there, framed in dusk light, his legs spread wide and his chest heaving. He lowered the first barrel of salt from his shoulder and rolled it into a corner. He carried in the second barrel and rolled it to the center of the room. Looking at Etheridge, he sat down squarely on the barrel. John Farrow poured him a brandy and Erskin sat quietly, warming it in his hands. Then, still looking at Etheridge, he spoke to George.

"The man in Philadelphia, lad, the man who needs a salt machine. What is his name?"

"Franklin," George replied. "Benjamin Franklin."

"And this Continental Army, these Americans who are fighting the men who killed our Hannah, what do they need?"

"Salt."

"No." Etheridge came halfway out of his chair. "You would not *give* the salt away."

"Shut up," Burrus said. "It is our salt."

Erskin silenced Burrus with his hand. "I don't know. I do know that our Austin is a man of property in Portsmouth. Important men dine at his table. Come now, Austin, tell us the latest news of this war."

5

"The horn, lad! Look to the horn!"

Conquering his stomach, George leaped forward to the prow of his father's fishing boat. He stood up, grateful for John Farrow's anchoring hand on his leg, took a great gulp of air, and sounded the beautifully curved, pink-and-white conch shell, asking permission to enter Portsmouth Harbor.

"Permission granted," the harbor master's horn, a foghorn bass growl, replied.

Just beyond the entrance buoys, atop a bottomless well of sludge-dark harbor water, a flotilla of great ships rode at anchor. Through bribery or bravado, they had broken the British blockade and now rode in challenge, gauntlet formation, to smaller, local craft. Air was trapped in pockets between the ships. Gleaming hulls rode tight together to stifle the smallest puff of wind. How would Erskin sail dead ahead, short-cut straight to anchor? Harbor regulations decreed that small sail take the longer route to the wharf.

Becalmed, Erskin waited just outside the buoys, tack line looped over his right hand, rudder in his left. The expression on his face willed wind, dared the faintest, peripheral breath to kiss his sails.

Farrow grinned. "If you would know how to sail," he said, "watch your father."

George and Farrow ducked out of the way, but George kept his head just high enough to see Portsmouth Town. A tremor ran through his body. No matter how many times he came into Portsmouth Harbor, it was always the first time. Always he was astonished anew by the tall houses, dizzingly high, shimmering, soaring into the sun. Even from a distance he could sense the energy that pulsed the people through the narrow, ballast-brick and cobblestone streets with running or dancing—never merely walking—momentum. Even sedate, stolid gentlemen, as sedate and stolid as Austin Etheridge, moved faster in Portsmouth. And ladies floated on air. In George's mind, ladies actually floated across Harbor Square and the parade green.

The wind came at last, teasing, tantalizing, a cool shadow on Erskin's face. George quickly lowered his head and lay flat on his back. The two sails did not move, but Erskin was transformed into a blur of action. His legs, long, lithe, became a second pair of hands. The heavy sails turned gossamer as a small, faint puff of wind wandered aimless as a fly into the cobweb of his skill.

"Small sail to port! Small sail to port!" The master's horn bleated a high, sharp warning.

At that moment the boat moved. There was suddenly so much wind, divine cheeks must have blown it. The boat began to fly. Erskin was no longer George's father or John Far-

46

row's best friend. Now zigzagging, now darting straight ahead like an enchanted arrow, Erskin sailed—past mercantile barques from Barbados, the fruit basket of the Caribbean, past passenger and cargo sloops from Portugal and Spain, French privateers, massive training square-riggers from the Netherlands.

George clutched his stomach and gaped as the world whirled by. Dutch boys, their bright blue caps set jauntily on masses of blond and blond-white curls, laughed and waved down to him. A bosun lifted his pipe in admiring salute. A Portuguese monkey, chained to a deck rail, indifferently scratched his armpits. Two gypsy women, their faces heavy with wine and sleep, stuck out their tongues. Overhead, so high, flags furled and snapped and ribboned a continuous rainbow against the sky. And Erskin sailed. Faster and faster.

Then there was no wind, none at all. The boat joined a mass of garbage in scudding and thumping quietly against the dock. Abruptly, feeling the breakfast he had not eaten churn up in his throat, George jumped ashore and fastened the towline to a cleat.

"Not bad for a yaupon eater," Farrow murmured as he helped Erskin lash the sails fast. Then as both men jumped ashore, he added, "Nor for the son of a yaupon eater. Let the boy be off now."

"It is his business today," Erskin replied, throwing a handful of coins to a group of gypsy children who threatened to bar their way, "as well as our own."

"Come now. Old Austin may be wrong. He had his gossip

47

about Colonel Campbell months ago. He may have vanished. Else been captured. Portsmouth is a nest of Tories."

Erskin looked at George. "It is his business. Come, lad, follow us."

George followed reluctantly, nearly running to keep up with his father. He might be old enough for Farrow's boat, but doubtless he would never be old enough to wander free in Portsmouth Town, to lose himself in noise and hurry and fantasy. He wanted to stay on the square forever, watching the carriages, the horsemen, the fortune tellers, and the pastry vendors. He wanted to buy a sack of ginger sticks and a green ribbon for Grizelle and a penny novel and a single-blade pocketknife with a mahoe-wood handle. Most of all, he wanted to walk past a certain address in the gypsy quarter. He wanted to see for himself if what Burrus Wahab said about a certain address was true.

Unfortunately, Erskin read his mind. Stopping in front of the cobbler's shop, Erskin said, "It's boots we came for and meeting Colonel Campbell. No other nonsense."

George, downcast but obedient, followed his father and Farrow to the cobbler's shop, the tack shop, the barber shop, and the tobacconist. And everywhere they met the refrain, "It's the war."

"No English leather these days. We're lucky to get Moroccan leather. Feeling is mountains high. In every occupied port, English leather rots in warehouses, beside English tea, English anything. It's the war. If you want the new hobnails. it'll cost extra."

"I've only an old razor to trim your beard, Captain Midgett.

Even gentlemen are sharpening English steel to slithers these days."

"No Turkish tobacco, sir. Only American. You'll smoke American if you smoke anything. Virginia bright leaf. Maryland burley. It's the war."

Erskin finally exploded in front of *The Polly Blue* Tavern. "The war! There was never a war in Portsmouth! Only pimps and profiteers and ex-pirates plundering ballroom society." He fingered the last silver coins in his pocket. He took out his watch and without looking at George, said to Farrow, "Noon less twenty minutes. Could we trust him to meet us here at noon?"

George laughed aloud, grabbed the money his father offered, and was off. The war might have caused shortages in Portsmouth, but the city still dazzled and tempted the greenhorn's eye. By half past noon George's money was gone and he had only one purchase to show for a mad dash into at least 16 shops. That one purchase was small enough to conceal in the deep, inside pocket of his sheepskin coat. He hadn't leftover money for a book, since penny novels were thruppence. Wearily, he turned toward *The Polly Blue*, grateful that he wouldn't be cheated there.

The Polly Blue sign, the head of a woman in a blue bonnet swinging gently in the wind, was actually the nameplate of a ship that had wrecked off Ocracoke Bar the first winter Erskin, George, and Hannah O'Neal had moved to Ocracoke. Led by Erskin, the islanders had pulled 28 survivors out of the storm, then salvaged the ship itself. To commemorate the unusual feat, the survivors arranged to build a tavern in

49

Portsmouth from the wrecked timber. Erskin volunteered the nameplate of *The Polly Blue*, his rightful prize. The names of the rescue team were inscribed on a bronze plaque on the tavern door. Any visitor from Ocracoke was awarded free room and board at *The Polly Blue*.

"George Midgett," he told the waiter, who ushered him to a corner table in the main dining room where his father and Farrow were waiting. In the smoky haze he saw dart players and dancing sailors.

"You're late." Erskin looked up. He was too big for the tavern facsimile of a captain's chair, his mutton chop was too fat, and the price of George's new boots and a can of tobacco still smarted deeply.

"It's the war." Farrow winked, passing George a tray of cold meat and bread and butter. "No roast beef or suckling pig, only mutton and tough tom turkey."

Starved, George considered it a feast. He ate three apple tarts, for which *The Polly Blue* was famous, and washed everything down with a large mug of dark ale. Erskin watched him without comment, drawing fitfully on a pipe.

"Colonel Campbell is here," Farrow said. "Has an office upstairs. He bears a hard grudge against the British. Very hard indeed. When old Austin gave up on the salt, he told us Campbell's story. The colonel will see us this afternoon."

George nodded. His father and Farrow had an urgent mission in Portsmouth: to see an acquaintance of Austin Etheridge, Colonel Charles Campbell, a quartermaster with the Continental Army. They had come to offer the army two

100-pound barrels of salt, by common consent a gift from the people of Ocracoke.

"Have you money enough for the puppet show?" Farrow asked, digging into his own pocket. "We'll meet you at the boat."

"He will stay with us," Erskin said.

"Oh, leave the boy. It is nothing for you and me to come to Portsmouth, but it is the boy's one holiday."

"The boy?" Erskin shook his head. "That will change, Farrow, when he has the place in your boat. He will earn his next pair of boots. I was married at his age. My name was scratched on this tavern door at nineteen. He will come with us."

His father spoke bluntly, matter-of-factly. The room went deadly quiet in George's mind. Every malevolent, mischievous eye seemed fixed on him. Blindly he stumbled after the two men, followed them through the lobby, down to the cellar, then up a flight of endless outside stairs, so dilapidated that each step creaked threateningly and some were missing altogether.

"Old Austin said he was a mole in a burrow." Farrow reached for George's hand. "Watch yourself."

Finally reaching what must have been the attic of *The Polly Blue*, his eyes adjusting to the dim light, George was aware of Colonel Campbell's importance. Many people were waiting to see him, patiently sitting on a long bench or leaning against the corridor wall: a lady in long gown and cape, merchants in black trousers and frock coats, a young Indian, bare-chested and wearing deerskin pants, with high cheek-bones and forehead shining like polished copper. Several boys, not much older than George, sagged against the wall, either too tired to stand upright or too proud to slump all the way to the floor.

"Continentals, I suspect," Farrow explained. "Soldiers fighting on the continent."

George felt sorry for them. They looked like ragged squirrels. Only one faintly resembled a soldier. He wore stained deerskin pants, a badly torn green jacket, and a coonskin cap.

"An outlander from the western mountains," Farrow said. "You can tell by the cap. No one on the Coast wears coonskin. Probably a courier. The outlanders can run faster than wild ponies."

"The Indian?"

"A Croatan. See the bear-claw tattoo on his chest? Doubtless come to barter venison and turpentine from Roanoke Island."

A large door, guarded by the one soldier armed with a rifle, opened at frequent intervals, yet it was an hour before Erskin and Farrow and George found a place on the bench. Erskin contented himself with his watch, placing it on his knee and opening the case. Farrow entertained George with the story of Charles Campbell.

"Old Austin didn't tell us the half of it," he began, "only that Campbell's vendetta against the British was personal, just as ours is. But the barmaid says Campbell's father sailed

with Blackbeard. Pirate money built the Campbell planta-
tion at Eden Town. Most of the money in Bath and Eden
Town is pirate money. Charles Campbell, the renegade's son
and our man, never turned his hand to a dark thing. So old
Austin says. He married a lady down to Savannah, from the
Oglethorpe colony, called Georgia now. He became a planter,
a tobacco planter."

"We'll wait five more minutes," Erskin said.

"It was taxes started the fracas," Farrow continued, "taxes
on rich men like Campbell and middle citizens. Oh, he
was rich soon enough and made friends to match his bank
account. It was the friends caused his trouble. First there
was Robert Caswell, the North Carolina governor, then the
Virginia governor, Patrick Henry. Campbell joined Caswell's
staff, a temporary appointment. When the fracas turned into
a war, Caswell moved his government from Bath to Halifax.
Campbell stayed behind. He wouldn't go because his wife
was sick."

"Five more minutes," Erskin said.

"The British sacked the coast of Pamlico Sound last year,"
Farrow continued. "Burned every house within seeing distance of their ships. Sent raiding parties ashore, too, only
those raids were after human game. Campbell's property was
at the top of the list. His friends were traitors, you see. Eat
at a friend's table, take his money at the whist table, and
you're a traitor. Campbell relied on Gentlemen's Code, whatever that is. He claimed to be neutral, to have no interest in
the war. His only interest was his wife's health.

"He went out to meet the raiding party, alone and unarmed. He told the officer his wife was dying. Even as he pleaded his case, the British fired his house, in front of his eyes, with his wife upstairs. He went half crazy. He pulled the officer off his horse—got his face slashed—but took the horse and rode clean away. The entire troop could find no trace of him. He later lost an eye to the officer's sword."

"It's two hours," Erskin said.

"His fighting days are done," Farrow continued. "He'd be hanged if he were captured. It takes nerve to be a Continental officer in Portsmouth. He's the only supply master left in a major port city. So keep your mouth shut. We wouldn't want our rumor to put him in chains."

Erskin stood up. "It's about time."

Farrow pushed George behind his father into the colonel's office. When the heavy door swung shut, George stayed in the back of the room.

His first thought was that nobody had ever called Colonel Charles Campbell "Charlie." He was a small, spare man, made even smaller by a very large desk. He was bald. A powdered wig hung on a wig stand behind the desk. He wore a plain blue coat and a plain white shirt with no collar. The desk was covered with papers. An inkwell holding two quill pens stood at his elbow. Other than the desk chair he sat in, there were no chairs or benches in the office. The only light came from a porthole-sized window to his left.

"Colonel Campbell." Erskin walked forward. "We are men of Ocracoke Island. A raiding party killed a woman in our village last week. We have come to offer a service to your army."

Silence.

"We have a provision of salt, sir. Two barrels of salt."

Silence.

"Two one-hundred pound barrels of salt. No brick or sand weight added."

Silence.

Erskin glanced back at Farrow, then moved closer and picked up the desk, holding it a good foot off the floor. Nothing moved on the desk surface. George watched the quill pens. Then he looked down. The small, spare man had small feet, clad in leather shoes that were as tattered and worn as George's old boots.

"Sir," the colonel spoke with great weariness, "would you kindly not do that?"

Erskin lowered the desk. "We are men—"

"I am so informed."

"We have salt—"

"How fortunate."

"The devil take you," Erskin spluttered.

"A long while ago, sir. The devil took me at an early age." The colonel looked up. One eye was covered with a black patch. The gaze from the good eye was all-encompassing. His overall bearing was so cold and pale, so condescending, that George shivered.

"So you offer me two barrels of salt for my army. But it is not your army?"

"We are fishermen, Colonel Campbell, not soldiers."

"Then I rather suspect you offer me two barrels of treachery. I have been fixed to this desk for five hours, besieged by spies, ruffians, and rum-soaked mercenaries. I don't trust my own mirror, sir. I certainly don't trust you."

Erskin fisted his hands but controlled himself. "I am not a ruffian. I am not a spy. I pulled that desk out of the sea, sir, and the rafters above, and every beam in this miserable tavern—"

"Please." The colonel raised his hand wearily. "Advertise proof of your masculinity within your own circle. It does not interest me. Your fellowship, perhaps, would be most welcome at another time in another place. Now, alas, I am tired and ill-humored. I have no pensions to offer wounded veterans who haunt every alley in Portsmouth. I have no consolation for a mother with a son on a prison ship. I have no defense against mercantile fleas who sold me watered wine. And I have no gold for two barrels of salt."

"The salt is not for sale," Erskin said. "It is a gift. It is retribution for murder."

The colonel returned to his papers. "While you are about it, give me also medicines, turpentine, blankets, tanned hides—" His voice trailed away. Then he spoke again, quietly. "Murder. I would know about murder." He looked up. "What is your name?"

"Midgett. Erskin Midgett. My friend John Farrow. My son George."

The colonel hesitated. "Midgett, eh. From Ocracoke. I have heard some talk of you."

Farrow stepped forward. "We were told, sir, that you are a quartermaster for the Continental Army."

"True."

"We were told that a major supply depot was in Portsmouth."

"True."

The colonel looked first to Erskin and then to Farrow. He waited a long moment. "Until a few months ago." He stood up and began to speak decisively and briskly. "Last year the blockade was a farce. At that time, in London clubs at least, there was no real war. We had little or no trouble in sending the general what he needed. General George Washington, the Continental commander. I knew him long ago, as a farmer. We exchanged tobacco plants.

"Then we began to score. We had great victories at Trenton and Princeton—battles won more by open supply lines than valor. No disrespect, but even now we have no trained, disciplined army. Washington leads by example and stamina. Last winter, victorious, he lost eight thousand men.

"Defeat is more costly, certainly with the Atlantic totally blocked. On land, we may be matched. On land, as rumor has it, the British fight with half a heart. Cornwallis, the British commander, considers this a civil war, brother against brother. The sea, however, is the British ace. A blockade spills no blood. It has merely starved and squeezed every port dry between Boston and Savannah."

The colonel stood up and moved to a large map on the wall behind his desk. "This winter is scarce begun and already the supply situation is critical. Washington is somewhere in Pennsylvania, presiding over what will be an army of living skeletons before spring. I don't know exactly where, but he is determined to stay within stinging distance of Philadelphia. But he can't hold without supplies. I am not at all hopeful. Nor is Governor Patrick Henry."

He returned to his desk, picked up a rolled document, and untied it. "This just came to me by courier. An enlistment poster newly endorsed by the Continental Congress. The Congress hasn't paid last year's bills. Yet read now what they propose to do." He held it out.

"I can't read," Erskin muttered. "But my son. . . ."

"The lad can read?" The colonel was surprised and beckoned George. "Come, lad. This is meant for boys like you."

George jerked forward, hoping his face wasn't smeared with apple tart. He began falteringly but gained confidence.

"Herewith, on this day, December 16th, 1777, the Continental Congress prescribes the following guarantees of service to each recruit in the Continental Army: two linen hunting shirts, two pairs stockings, two pairs shoes, two pairs overalls, one leather or woolen jacket, one pair breeches, one leather hat or cap. The daily ration shall include one pound beef, pork, or salt fish, one pound bread or flour, one pint milk, one quart beer or cider, with a weekly ration of beans and other vegetables, rice or Indian meal, candles, and soap."

"Aye, you can read." The colonel looked at him very directly and George felt an odd premonition as he returned the document. "But what propaganda, what pap." The colonel crumpled the poster in disgust. "The Congress also knows, using a projection of last year's figures, that half of Washington's army, some eleven thousand men, will desert, freeze, or starve to death unless we circumvent the blockade. And that, I fear, is a conservative estimate."

Now he walked to the small window. "Out there, on the Portsmouth dock, is a cornucopia. What I cannot buy, I can arrange to steal. Tons of supplies—with your salt a most valuable addition. Everything I need is out there. But I can't move it. Gentlemen, I couldn't move two barrels of salt across Harbor Square, much less anything else. What I most need, the most important service, is not to be found in Portsmouth."

"You only need overland transport," Erskin said. "The sea is not the only highway to Pennsylvania."

"Oh?" The colonel returned to the map. "Not the sea, eh, but overland. You think I am blinkered to the sea, when the rivers and plains of the inland tidewater are at my disposal." He spoke with bitter sarcasm. "You think I should go here, in a direct line to Pennsylvania—from here, on the Pamlico Coast, to here, the Delaware River. The area has never been charted, and the distance must be more than three hundred miles."

"The area you speak of is the Great Dismal Swamp," Farrow said. "Erskin and I know the waters up to the swamp. But any Croatan Indian could get through the swamp blindfolded."

"Oh?" the colonel repeated. "And then what? Where? To Suffolk? Once through the swamp, the barge still has a long way to go. . . ."

59

"A barge?" Erskin asked. "What kind of barge?"

"A boat with sail and poles," the colonel said quietly, "that is also a wagon with a mule team."

Farrow looked at Erskin, then spoke confidently. "We are unlettered, sir, but we are not without other skills. We build our own boats and houses on Ocracoke. Storms plague us, but they do not destroy us. With seasoned timber and proper caulking, and with mule-team way stations, such a barge could go anywhere."

Colonel Campbell returned to his desk and sat down heavily. "I, too, would have thought so. I had supposed that runaway slaves would do anything for freedom, or Portsmouth gypsies anything for a price. Enough gold, I falsely hoped, would stimulate courage enough to survive the swamp, the distance, and the winter. But I was wrong."

"You have already tried it?" Erskin said.

"Twice. I lost one barge to the black market in Suffolk. The second never left Portsmouth. One night it was guarded and manned by twelve frontiersmen, the best marksmen and most trustworthy soldiers I know. The next morning it was stripped bare. Obviously, the barge must be built and loaded outside Portsmouth. But I cannot risk a third try." He hesitated. "Or can I?"

Erskin looked at Farrow. Farrow looked at Erskin.

"But we are fishermen," Erskin protested. "Ocracoke is a small village. Even two men would be sorely missed. It might be February before a barge could reach Pennsylvania."

"February." The colonel nodded. "With luck and a push from God's own hand."

6

Although the church was cold and the pew bench hard, the bench would have felt as soft as a goose-down mattress if George had stretched out. He had never been so tired. After lighting the fire laid in the hearth behind the altar, he moved to the back of the church. The warming fire would put him to sleep.

He could not sleep, not on this, his guard watch. Pride joined duty to keep him alert. Everyone knew he had done his share, more than his share. Even his father had noticed it. No one in the village had worked harder to make the barge exactly what Colonel Campbell had specified. George had always been good with his hands. Hannah O'Neal had known he could fix anything. Now the village knew it, too.

The village had balked when Erskin and John Farrow returned from Portsmouth Town. Two barrels of salt was gift and retribution enough. Ballance Meekins had already spoken for the timber from Hannah's farmhouse to build a house for his bride. And Mollie Wahab had put her foot down about using the church as a storeroom. The church was a sanctuary. If the church was to be turned into a warehouse, then common consent might just as well return the silver candlesticks Mollie had donated to the altar. Mollie's candlesticks would not be a part of Colonel Campbell's plan.

George smiled. For some strange reason, in the dusk light falling dark, shadowing the supplies stacked high against the walls, the place had never felt more like a church. All the grumbling, the dissent, the frustration that had threatened to turn the village upside down had ended here—in the church. And it had ended very quickly.

Timber from Hannah O'Neal's farmhouse had been transformed into the barge that now waited at the dock. Every joint was tight and smooth, every seam caulked secure. Long, cumbersome, ungainly, sitting as flat and awkward in the water as a loggerhead turtle squatting to lay eggs, nothing about it was beautiful. But it had not been built for the open sea. It had been built for a long haul through stagnant swamp and inland wilderness. Men, not the wind, would pole it forward. Mules, not the tide, would propel it to a landlocked place in Pennsylvania. Unlike other large or small sail, nothing about it was beautiful, graceful, inviting, or mysterious.

George thought it all these things. He had turned the joints to which the removable wagon wheels would be fixed. He had deciphered the squiggles on Colonel Campbell's diagram and fixed the wheel spokes exactly six inches apart. Unknown to anyone, he had carved his initials at the top of the short masthead, fitted with a small, square sail. He was proud of what he had done.

Because he could read, he had spent long hours in the

public house every night, poring over the soundings charts and maps and written instructions that arrived by courier from the office atop *The Polly Blue* Tavern. Everything had to be memorized, for Colonel Campbell's first order was that every written communication had to be burned.

Yet Erskin Midgett and John Farrow did not know how to follow orders. They had spent their lives giving orders, making the instant decisions on which their livelihood or life itself depended. On the surface, John Farrow might display kindness and a sense of humor. Underneath he was as stubborn and tenacious as a nor'easter. Only Erskin Midgett could tell John Farrow what to do. This was rare, because John Farrow instinctively knew what to do. Obedience was even more alien to Erskin. Jenny Scarborough had long ago given up the simple instruction on how to use a napkin. So Erskin glowered and paced the floor of the public house and wondered aloud if the colonel weren't a little cracked.

"Damn his bureaucratic soul. I'll wager he never set foot in a boat in his life, or a barge, or whatever that thing is we're supposed to build. Nor will I follow an Indian through the Great Dismal Waste."

"Johnny Locklear," George read from the colonel's letter. "A Croatan. He'll come here, to Ocracoke, at the appointed time." He looked up. "You told the colonel an Indian could go through the Great Dismal blindfolded."

"So you did," Farrow muttered. "Following the Indian doesn't bother me. It's that everlasting 'at the appointed time.' We're past the Dismal and into Suffolk, Virginia, and at the appointed time someone will meet us with the team

63

of mules. We wait at Suffolk until the appointed time. Who will meet us? How long will we wait? Days, perhaps. I don't like it, Erskin. He orders us hither and yon—but where exactly? I say he has a strange notion of trust."

"His notion of trust is complete distrust," Erskin said. He leaned over George's shoulder and gazed at the map. "Suffolk. Then where? To Morris Liston's Land, somewhere on the Potomac Bay. Then where? Somebody will meet you at the appointed time. What's this, lad? Is this Pennsylvania? What's this mark?"

"An iron forge," George said. "Maybe thirty miles from Philadelphia. It's the location of an iron forge."

"And that's where we're going?"

"Yes." George thought of Moncie Scarborough and how he had been bound for an ironmonger's job in Philadelphia.

"On blind faith," Erskin muttered. "Somebody will meet us. Highwaymen, no doubt. We'll be carrying enough provisions to found a new colony, and some phantom will meet us."

"No wonder his previous expeditions failed," Farrow complained. "If I have to fight this war, I'd sooner shoulder a rifle and join the army. See here, the Indian stays behind in Suffolk? He's still there when we return?"

"No," George said. "Somebody else will meet you."

Farrow smiled grimly as the papers curled to ash in the hearth. "I am not sure, Erskin, that I have courage enough for the colonel's foolishness."

"We pledged our word," Erskin said slowly. "We made a promise in the heat and hurt of Hannah's death."

George saw worry in his father's eyes. Pacing the floor,

his temper flaring high, Erskin was not the brash giant who had picked up the colonel's desk. His uncertainty was contagious. Days passed, and no one lifted a finger to dismantle the farmhouse and begin the barge. When the supplies began to arrive from Portsmouth Town, via small blockade runners, Erskin reluctantly stored them in the church and said only, "There's nowhere else to store them. Our salt multiplies like five loaves and two fishes."

Suddenly, everything changed. Overnight, if Colonel Charles Campbell had asked the entire village to journey to the far side of the moon, the people would have done so. The givers of two 100-pound barrels of salt themselves received a gift.

Shipwreck timber had built the church, strong seasoned timber that, barring a gale, would stand forever. The outside structure had been completed, the altar, pew benches, and arch frame for the front door cut, when the timber ran out. Wood of the same kind and thickness ran short. There was no wood for a door that would properly herald the entrance to God's House. The villagers cut several doors from green pine which, after they warped, rotted out. Every attempt to fit a church door had turned into a reproach against bad planning. For two years, either a gaping hole or the wrong kind of door blighted community spirit. Nor could the villagers, including Austin Etheridge, bring themselves to pray for the beneficence of another wreck.

Then, on an unusually cold and windy morning in late December, a door washed up. *The* door. Out of the sea mist, into the harbor calm, onto the beach. Although covered with barnacles and weed, it was perfectly proportioned, of the same wood and thickness as the original church timber. Also included were wrought-iron latches and hinges. Burrus Wahab found it. Burrus, who had favored the colonel's plan, proclaimed it an omen. The men carried it from the beach, scraped it, hinged it, and hung it. It was made for no other church in the world. It was *the* door.

Mollie Wahab returned the candlesticks. Erskin left off damning the colonel's bureaucratic soul. Everyone got down to business. In two weeks' time, the barge thumped solidly against the dock. With the arrival of Johnny Locklear from Roanoke Island, the barge would be loaded, the supplies lashed tight under heavy canvas waterproofed with bear grease, and Erskin and John Farrow would be gone.

Numb with cold, watching shadows deepen as the time neared for evening service and the end of his guard watch, George checked the supplies: the salt, bundles of tanned hides, woolen blankets, 100 pairs of leather boots, two casks of rum, and a large chest of medicines, including turpentine and laudanum, an opium-based pain-killer—all destined for the long journey.

George wondered how the village would fare without the two best men, his father and Farrow, in the dead of winter. Would Hannah O'Neal have approved such sacrifice? The fire's warmth did not touch him in the dark recesses of the church. His father had never left him before.

There had been whale hunts and days of deep-sea fishing and trips to Portsmouth Town. There had been storms and wrecks and long nights of danger. But his father had always come home. Shrugging off peril as though it were commonplace, quick to credit another's endurance but never his own, Erskin lived each day with reckless energy. And he had always come home. George felt an odd loneliness. He realized, achingly, that his father might not come back. So many men had not come back.

George had not even faced the months ahead. His father had been too busy to tell him what to do in his absence.

"I could mend your net," George said.

"Aye, son, you could do that."

"Burrus Wahab's cistern needs new bricking."

"So it does. You could do that."

"Venison. With you and Farrow gone, I'll go deer hunting up to Hatteras."

"Aye. Why not?"

A light flickered on the church altar. Someone had come in the back way and was lighting the candlesticks from a taper from the fire. George came instantly alert when he saw Grizelle Scarborough. George didn't move.

A tall, rather slender girl, she had Jenny's dark eyes and a mass of dark hair inherited from her father. She had beautiful hands, George thought, watching them reflected in the candlelight. She looked very fragile and very young and something in her face was always smiling—not an open smile, but an inner glow, as though some secret knowledge amused her.

Grizelle thrust her long cape aside, smoothed the folds of her white dress, and reached behind the altar for a dulcimer, a harp set in an oblong, soundboard box. She sat down on the altar bench and, face profiled in his direction, played a series of soft chords. With a start, George realized that it was Christmas—the eleventh day of Christmas. The villagers celebrated Old Christmas, as people had done since the Middle Ages, beginning on December 24 and going on for 12 days. Tomorrow was the Epiphany, the day of the arrival of the Magi at the Bethlehem cradle, the first proof of the divinity of the Christ Child and the most glorious day in Christendom. He had forgotten all about it.

In a high, clear voice, Grizelle practiced the Epiphany hymn for the service.

"Saw you never in the twilight
When the sun had left the skies
Up in heaven clear stars shining
Through the gloom like silver eyes?
So of old the wise men watching
Saw a little stranger star
And they knew the King was given
And they followed it from far."

Did he have the nerve? The gift was there, deep in his pocket. It had been in his pocket since he bought it in Portsmouth Town—a tiny silver locket on a green ribbon—a heart-shaped silver locket. He had been a fool to buy it. It was too personal a gift. A heart!

There was just time before the service for a big lie. He would tell her he had got it from a gypsy woman in Portsmouth, got it for practically nothing. Found it on the street perhaps, just lying on the street, and had bought the ribbon to match it. A ribbon wasn't so personal.

But there was no time. He stepped forward and took his place at the back bench as the front door opened and Mollie and Burrus Wahab led the villagers into the church. Some of them carried small candles.

Grizelle strummed the chords a little louder.

"Heard you never of the story
How they crossed the desert wild
Journeyed on by plain and mountains
Till they found the Holy Child?
How they opened all their treasure,
Kneeling to that infant king,
Gave the gold and fragrant incense
Gave the myrrh in offering?"

The villagers had no gold, fragrant incense, or myrrh. Instead, they had greater treasures for the soldiers in faraway Pennsylvania. While the barge had been hammered and nailed, the women had been knitting sweaters, socks, and scarves. The tradition of giving to each other had not been followed this year. All the gifts were for the soldiers. One by one the women brought their knitted goods to the altar. Then the men came forward and offered hand-carved pipes and packets of precious tobacco.

"Know ye not that lowly baby
Was the bright and morning star,
He who came to light the desert
And the darkened isles afar?"

The church filled with an outpouring of music and love. George was suddenly warm. He felt his eyes sting. He would never tell another lie. When everything was over, after the excitement of departure, he would find Grizelle and tell her the truth. "Look, I saw this in a Portsmouth shop and it reminded me of you, and I want you to have it. Merry Christmas."

> "And we, too, may seek His cradle,
> There our hearts' best treasures bring,
> Love and faith and true devotion
> For our Saviour, God, and King."

His father and Burrus Wahab stood at the altar. When the villagers had rustled into place, George heard the door latch click. Treading on a thick and sudden silence, an Indian appeared in the back of the church. Everyone turned to see him.

This was Johnny Locklear, the signal. The barge would be loaded that night. George inwardly groaned. Again he would get no sleep. He might never sleep again. The Indian turned slightly and looked directly at him. George recognized the bear tattoo on his upper chest, although now he wore a heavy deerskin jacket. It was the same man he had seen in the corridor outside Colonel Campbell's office.

"All rise," Burrus Wahab intoned. "All rise to bless the mission of this village and to ask that our men, Erskin Midgett and John Farrow, be kept journey safe and journey proud. All rise."

Erskin put an authoritative hand on his shoulder.

"I ask all to be seated."

Confused, the villagers sat down.

"I have given long thought to this decision," Erskin began. "I have considered the penalty of taking two able-bodied men from our village. Not only are you cheated of your pork provision, but with both me and Farrow away, you are deprived of your two best huntsmen and fishermen. You gave me the responsibility for the salt. I now accept the responsibility for my absence. John Farrow is my trusted friend. He is also husband to Mary and father to a new child. Every man here has a family, to whom he is first beholden. I would not have Farrow leave his family. He will stay here. I can depend on no other man to guide you through the winter."

Erskin waited a moment. "I have no family, only my son, who is of age. He has pulled his oar with the building of the barge. My son will go with me. Now, all rise and we will receive your blessing."

George found himself moving up the aisle, both proud and puzzled by his father's announcement. He had so often prayed that his father might believe in him. Then he heard the snigger, the small, quickly hushed snigger of laughter. He knew it was Ballance Meekins. He knew it wasn't Grizelle Scarborough. Somehow he knew that.

The candles were so bright, exploding into wide bursts in his eyes. Both his father's and Burrus Wahab's hands came down on his shoulders. Hearing Burrus intone the last blessing, George looked out at the people of his life and was more alone, and more afraid, than he had ever been before.

7

Leaning far overboard, splashing handfuls of icy water over his face, trying not to puke into the wind, George again wondered: why was he here? Why was his father so crazy?

A soft, low snuffle offered sympathy. George cupped his mouth with his hands and whistled. The porpoises were still there, leading the way. He watched the great black humps rise and fall, arc and dive, snuffle and whoosh and answer his whistle. Morning light touched the black-and-gray bodies, silvered and streaked them with brilliant greens and blues. George had seen porpoises before, but never so many and never so close. Fifty porpoises, perhaps more, moved steadily on, escorting the barge through the vast inland sea that was Pamlico Sound.

The loss of home cut deeper. No longer was there a trace of wandering Portsmouth sloops or longboats. No sign of land anywhere. The barge had moved at full sail past familiar landmarks: Kinnakeet Banks where Erskin and George had been born, Chicamacomico where pirates had buried both bodies and treasure. Ahead lay Croatan Sound and

Roanoke Island, Johnny Locklear's home. George now saw nothing but a bright, winter sea, nauseating and endless.

Johnny came up silently, without warning. George jumped. Johnny was everywhere on the barge, which grew smaller as the sound grew wider. He was a constant shadow falling between Erskin at the rudder and George at the bow, rarely speaking but always there. Erskin, too, had hardly spoken since the voyage began. Was it his sickness, George wondered, or resentment of Johnny that kept Erskin's mood so dark?

Johnny held out a square of chewing tobacco.

"No, thank you."

"Not tobacco. Bark. From the root tree, the Hercules root. It will keep your breakfast in your stomach."

George hesitated. The bark chewed bitter at first, then sweet. He swallowed the juice and spat out the pulp.

"The better the sailor," Johnny said, "the worse the sickness."

Johnny's dark eyes were set in a long face the color of gold. He wore his black hair long in the back and short on the side, a band of white coral beads circling his forehead. But it was his long coat that fascinated George—a beaver coat, with the fur turned inside, and a complete pelt, including the beaver's head and whiskers, as a hood. Johnny used the coat as a blanket at night, his head nestled against the beaver's glass-bead eyes.

"You must eat more than tea and bread."

"I can't keep anything down."

"You will now."

73

Johnny cooked breakfast over the sand fire, a bucket of sand soaked in whale oil that served as a stove. He sizzled a fresh blue he had speared and cleaned but set aside a raw portion for himself. George was amazed at the power of the bark. He could hardly wait to get the hot fish into his mouth, to peel and swallow the Portsmouth oranges almost whole, to gobble the fresh bread that Mollie Wahab had packed in the pantry chest.

"I have seen bigger fish," Erskin said when George carried him his plate. "Tell the Indian the Pamlico is famous for big blues."

George didn't tell Johnny anything. It annoyed him that Erskin never spoke for himself. What was the matter with him? Jealousy of Johnny? George raked the sand fire clean and stowed the scarred old pewter plates in the chest. At least Erskin would find no fault with his housekeeping. Let him spend another day in silence, seemingly asleep, with his right hand and foot on the rudder that no one else could touch.

And let Johnny sit on the barrels of salt, crouched, quiet and watchful and mysterious. He was earning ten guineas, five paid at Portsmouth and five to be paid at the rendezvous in Suffolk. George wanted to ask Johnny so many things: why he ate fish raw, what lay ahead in the Great Dismal Swamp, why he worked for Colonel Campbell. But George was not experienced in first moves. Sadly, he thought of the locket on the green ribbon he had bought for Grizelle, pressed mute and useless in a book.

George took his knife and began work on the poles. He cut

deep gashes about three feet from the bottom of the long, 20-pound pine logs. When the water line came up to that mark, the pole was sunk deep enough into the mud to push the barge forward.

"Let me help you."

Although George was proud of his skill, Johnny's knife was sharper and cut deeper faster.

"A journey is easy," Johnny said, "in the beginning. When we go out on a hunting party, we only work when we are hungry. Only then do we find a bear or deer. The same now. The weather is too warm, the sky too blue, the Pamlico too tame. The crabs should be buried in winter sleep, but I see them walking just under the surface. . . . Land." Johnny pointed to the horizon. "Roanoke Island."

The name George had memorized slowly came alive—a green island with cedars and pines and holly, a narrow brown beach. Erskin took advantage of the high-tide flow through Croatan Sound to get into Albemarle Sound as darkness fell.

"My home," Johnny said wistfully. "I have not seen my family for six months. My wives and children."

"How many wives?" George's eyes brightened with curiosity.

"Not in the English way," Johnny replied, "not chained to one woman forever by the church. Everyone is your family in my land. No woman is without a father, a brother, a husband. No child is without a mother and father. Everyone has food and water, unless all are hungry and thirsty."

George sensed that Johnny was lonely and homesick.

75

Quietly, he moved his deerskin bed closer. He lay on his back, watching stars. The night was cold, but his feet were warm and supper secure in his stomach. He could smell Erskin's pipe and hear the porpoises splash. He could also hear oysters spitting on the nearby mud flats of the sound.

"Roanoke Island is your home and you are a Croatan," George ventured timidly. "I have heard about the English settlers who came here long ago and were lost. Do you know about them?"

"Those people were never lost," Johnny replied. "Never. Do you want to hear the story?"

"Yes. I had a friend once, Henry Frampton, a man I helped through shipwreck fever. He told me the colony disappeared." How he envied Johnny's coat, and the band of coral beads that shone in the darkness, and the way he sat on his heels for hours.

"The truth is why I have an English name, Locklear," Johnny began. "The truth has been handed down in the Croatan family for many years.

"It began with an English sea captain named Grenville. He was a friend of the Elizabeth queen, the first woman to sit on your throne. Grenville came to Roanoke Island looking for gold. The French had been here, and the Spanish, and the Portuguese, but there never was any gold. Grenville found only the Croatans and tobacco.

"He didn't want to go home empty-handed. He took many hogsheads of tobacco and two Croatan brothers. They were young boys, very beautiful and strong, named Wanchese and Manteo. Wanchese was the older, dark-eyed and suspicious in character. Manteo was a happy boy with a warm, open nature.

"Wanchese and Manteo weren't taken as prisoners. They wanted to go, to cross the great sea. I would have gone, too. Imagine sailing as guests on an English ship, meeting the Elizabeth queen, seeing London, being invited into the homes of lords and ladies. They had a good time, even if they were looked on as . . . curiosities. . . ."

"Freaks," George put in. "Like us, the people of Ocracoke. We are called queer because we are yaupon eaters."

"Yes." Johnny nodded. "Wanchese and Manteo came safely home, but like most people who travel the same road, they quarreled about what they had seen.

"Wanchese didn't trust the English. He said they would come to Roanoke Island by the hundreds, then by the thousands, and take our land, destroy our way of life. He said the English had no land of their own. No matter their promises or treaties, they would drive us into darkness. Wanchese was a prophet of doom.

"Manteo said the opposite. He said many good, hardworking people in England wanted to come to Roanoke Island, but they were afraid of the Croatans. Manteo didn't want these people to be afraid. He wanted the English to settle the big cities, like Suffolk and Portsmouth, and let the Croatans farm and hunt and trade with them. Together they would build a new community. Together they would fight the Skeets and Corees, the Spanish and French and Portuguese. Manteo was a prophet of hope.

"Wanchese and Manteo argued so violently about the

future that they went to war. Families fought each other over the English, who were not here, who were thousands of miles away, who did not know or care about us.

"Manteo won. Wanchese retreated to the southern corner of the island and died of despair. Manteo waited for his new English friends.

"They finally came, family men with wives, and they came to stay. Sir Walter Raleigh, a great captain and the Elizabeth queen's friend, arrived with one hundred and twelve settlers—men, women, and children. They were the first American colony. They built homes and a church, plowed land and planted crops. They weren't many people, compared to Manteo's community, but the Croatans did everything possible to make them feel at home.

"The names are still remembered—Brownlee and White, Smith and Wheelwright, Fearing and Locklear. One family was named Dare—Ananias and Elenor Dare. Elenor was the daughter of John White, who served under Raleigh. A baby girl was born to the Dares shortly after they arrived. They named her Virginia, after Elizabeth, supposedly a virgin. Sir Walter said the queen would be pleased with the name.

"After Raleigh sailed away—no one knows exactly when—a storm hit the barrier reefs that protect us. Roanoke Island is so big, with so many trees and dunes of grass, that no one worried. Even the biggest storms usually blow out in Pamlico Sound. But this storm didn't die. Water came over the highest dunes. Manteo ordered everyone to leave.

"Our people sometimes do this—move to the continent until the danger has passed. Always they returned. But this time they couldn't. The island was covered with water by the storm. A scout returned in a canoe and reported that nobody could go back. The beach was washed away. Forests were blown down. All the houses, including the sacred burial house, were gone. The scout carved the name—CROATAN—on one tree that stood above the water.

"Everyone then faced the same unknown continent. Some traveled far west, to the land of the Cherokees. Others went south, to the Oconees and Catabaws. The Croatans and their English neighbors were never lost. They were survivors."

"Like us," George said. "We are survivors on Ocracoke Island. Why do you think people now believe Croatans killed the settlers?"

"Because Sir Walter Raleigh never meant to come back. The settlers were a bad investment. How could they send him a return on his money? How much tobacco, corn, or timber? Raleigh left them stranded.

"John White spent three years trying to return to his daughter and granddaughter. He was crazed with worry. When he finally raised the funds, he didn't stay long. How could White persuade his sailors to spend months looking for a people who had vanished? He only found the name CROATAN on the tree.

"Raleigh's guilty conscience blamed the Croatans. Why not? While Raleigh was sailing for gold in the Caribbean, Manteo was protecting the settlers with his life. He and the Virginia baby were baptized in the same church. Manteo had staked his own future on the colony's success. He had to save everyone or no one. He saved everyone from the storm."

79

"Manteo was right," George said sleepily. "It was right to be friendly. Wanchese was wrong."

"I no longer believe in either one. Only myself. It is like this war now, between you and your brothers, between English friends. Just as Wanchese fought Manteo."

I'm not fighting anyone, George thought, closing his eyes on the overhead stars, giving in to the snuffle lullaby around the boat.

Morning was a soft, stealthy pink, filtering through fog, turning leafless trees into pink skeletons. The mirror water was stained ink black by tannic acid, oozing from the roots of cypress trees. The water smelled of death, of dying plants, the rotten-egg odor of sulphur. The quiet was too quiet, jarringly broken by the screech of an owl or the stupid honk of a pelican. A murmuring whir of insects overlaid the quiet, an eternal one-note hum that was neither major nor minor, never resolving, so loud that George could hear nothing else, so soft he strained to hear it. The leaden mist was hard to breathe.

"He's gone. The Indian. Your friend."

George saw the beaver coat, neatly folded.

"He'll be back." George scrambled toward the echo distortion of Erskin's voice. "He left his coat. We're in the swamp, the Great Dismal," George whispered with awe and excitement.

"Hell, more likely." Erskin hungrily ate his breakfast of sturgeon roe and toasted bread, reached for his rum and pipe.

The sudden thud of Johnny's return knocked the pipe from Erskin's mouth. Johnny swung down from an overhead poplar, two headless wild turkeys strung on his belt. Laughing, squatting in front of Erskin's rage, he plucked and gutted the turkeys and laid the plump dark meat on top of the pantry chest.

"We shall eat now," Johnny said proudly, washing his hands in the black water. "Really eat. Turkey and pheasant and turtle and sweet herbs and berries—"

Erskin swore. "You are paid to move this barge, not swing around like an ape."

Johnny winked at George. "I planned our way this morning, walking through the trees. We shall move slowly this first day. You have never poled before. I will show you."

"I have poled before. You can teach the boy."

"The poles are our wind and sail." Johnny ignored him. "You will take the left pole, George the right. I will steer from the back. When we find islands of land, you and I will be mules, Captain Midgett. We will harness ourselves with rope and pull the barge."

The one-note hum of the insects thundered in George's ears. Overnight, Johnny was in command. He would steer from the back.

"It is near noon, Locklear. You have wasted half the day."

"I wasted half a day to save us three days looking for food." Nothing broke Johnny's happy mood. He moved to Erskin's place at the back, raised his pole, and thrust it deep into the water until he struck mud. Erskin and George took up their stations. Looking ahead, George saw a family of raccoons, father, mother, and two cubs, peering from the hollow of a tree. They were a skeptical audience.

George set to with everything he had: hands toughened in salt water, a calm stomach, desperate determination. The barge creaked, moved with an easy glide.

Erskin was born to any task that required strength and rhythm. Each time he set his pole, the barge took flight. George marveled at the muscular strength that rippled across Erskin's shoulders and down his legs. Nor would he stop.

George marked the time by the touch of Johnny's hand on his shoulder. That meant rest, eat, and drink. But Erskin never stopped—only when dusk turned pitch dark.

Johnny disappeared every night. George wondered where he went and what he did.

"There is a lake the day after tomorrow," Johnny announced. "Then you can raise sail again, Captain Midgett. But I want a day to scout. Let George go with me. The two of us can cover more ground."

"Are you lost, Locklear?"

"I will find the fastest way to the lake," Johnny replied evenly.

"Then go alone. Mark your trail on the trees. George and I will follow the marks."

It was Erskin who was lost, George reflected. Even though Colonel Campbell had personally chosen Johnny as their guide, it was almost impossible for Erskin to surrender his independence, especially to a young Indian.

"Remember what I warned you about," Johnny told George before he disappeared in the night.

Johnny had warned him about so many things. Goblin roots. Poisonous snakes. Wild pigs and boars. What else? What other dangers lay ahead of them in this wild, Godforsaken swamp?

George poled from the front of the barge and called out directions according to the trees Johnny had notched.

"Don't push so hard," George called back to his father. Johnny had told him it was balance, not force, that kept the barge moving on an even keel. But with Johnny gone, Erskin was trying to outdo himself.

"You can push harder, son," Erskin yelled. "Let's show Locklear what we can do."

You're a fool, George thought angrily. If he didn't match Erskin's stroke, the barge would capsize, and he would be blamed. Desperately, he pushed harder and faster, and suddenly punched a hole in air. The pole plunged into deeper nothingness. George would not let the pole go. He tried to climb it. Mud seeped into his boots. Black water covered his head. The water was warm and evil-smelling. And Johnny had warned him about quicksand. Why couldn't he struggle? He liked the quiet, dark cradle of mud.

His head almost exploded when he was pulled free. He was roped to Johnny who was roped to Erskin who was roped to the mast. The only thing he knew, as his bare stomach scraped across the deck of the barge, was that he had lost his boots.

"Thank God you saw him fall. Keep his head up."

Erskin's anguish echoed from what seemed miles away.

"I was watching him, Locklear." Erskin untied the rope around George's shoulders and chest. "I was watching him and he was just . . . gone."

As George came to, he saw his father and Johnny glaring at each other. He had swallowed a little quicksand mud but now spat most of it out.

"You pushed him too hard, Captain Midgett. He knows he is small and not strong, but you make him smaller. I wanted him to go with me, to relax, to see the birds and animals."

Erskin wiped the mud from George's face.

"He has been cooped up too long in your pride and anger," Johnny continued.

"That's enough, Locklear. I did push him too hard, and you have saved his life. I will be ever thankful. Please join me in a rum and pipe."

George welcomed his father's truce, watched him pour mugs of rum. It was the best Erskin could do. Hunkering down in his bed, aching in every bone, George smiled. The long silence between his father and his friend was over.

The barge moved on, steady on. Erskin and Johnny pulled the barge when they found moss and leaf-covered ground. Erskin never again told George to push harder. He seemed pleased when George slipped away at dusk with Johnny. And George, curious and newly bold, slipped away from Johnny.

Once he came on a small clearing and saw something so

remarkable, so wonderful, he choked with laughter. A raccoon was kissing a deer. The raccoon stood on his hind legs, embraced the fawn with his front paws, and dreamily kissed the fawn's left eye. The fawn's floppy ears went straight up. The raccoon's black-moon eyes closed tight in ecstasy. The fawn, black nose twitching, looked straight at George with resignation.

At night, Erskin and Johnny swapped stories around the sand fire, the truth finally fading into lies. Erskin had killed a shark. Johnny had killed a bear. Erskin told of the wreck of *The Polly Blue*, the 28 people he had pulled from a hurricane surf. Johnny told of Skeet and Coree war parties, of how he had killed 30 enemies. Erskin told of storms that lifted houses from one village to another and set them down without breaking a teacup. Johnny told of harvests with 50-pound pumpkins, of hunting parties that brought back three tigers.

"What did you see today?" Erskin asked George.

"A raccoon kissing a deer."

"That is what you would see." Erskin nodded fondly.

They came at last to the large lake that Johnny had so accurately scouted. Erskin raised the square sail and the barge shuddered free, settled into the fresh, lake water and moved on. Once across the lake, they would meet the men from Suffolk.

"The porpoises told us good-bye in Albemarle Sound," Johnny said, wrapping his coat around his shoulders. "Very soon, whistling swans will welcome you to Chesapeake Bay."

George, hearing the night music, watching the night colors of phosphorus and fireflies, saw Johnny pull the beaver face hood around his head. Johnny was only guiding them to Suffolk. Johnny, too, would say good-bye.

"Why do you eat raw fish?" George asked.

Johnny reached in the pocket of his coat and brought out pieces of Hercules root. He pressed the bark into George's hand.

"You will need this on the Chesapeake."

"Why do you eat raw fish?"

Johnny smiled patiently. "I don't see what you see. I don't hear what you hear. I don't feel what you feel. You and I are different. If we respect that difference, I'll never ask why you eat cooked fish."

The barge turned into a wagon for the first time on the solid ground beyond the lakeshore. George happily directed the fixing of the wheels, since he had engineered and built them. Then Erskin and Johnny pulled the wagon to the rendezvous point with the men and mules from Suffolk. Johnny gathered wood for the morning fire.

George wakened to the sweet smell of hickory smoke, not surprised to see Erskin alone by the fire. Johnny had vanished during the night, but George had promised to find him again in Portsmouth, when the mission was over.

Two men, each leading a mule, came out of the woods and walked toward Erskin. They carried rifles and large knapsacks. George looked, and looked again. Something was wrong, terribly wrong.

"Erskin Midgett? I am Crowell, Reuben Crowell, and this

is Mathew Reeve. We have brought the mules, Captain, and Morris Liston's compliments. You are welcome to Suffolk and Morris Liston's land."

Erskin lit his pipe with a splinter from the fire.

"We had not expected you on time, Captain. Only birds fly through the Dismal."

George ran toward his father. Why was Reuben Crowell wearing Johnny's coat?

8

"Yes, we shot Locklear, Captain Midgett," Crowell was saying. "We thought we'd killed Locklear last month, when we caught him running rifles and shot out of Suffolk to the Cherokees."

"Give the boy the coat," Erskin replied.

"We had true men a year ago," Reeve said. " 'Twasn't as it is now. Everybody was true. The Indians took no side then. The Tories we'd killed or driven to Canada."

"The coat," Erskin repeated.

"A boy like you,"—Crowell shrugged out of the coat and gave it to George—"spindly and shivering blue, would need this coat. Take it. Can we move now, Captain Midgett?"

Erskin didn't reply, his face dark and threatening.

"Captain," Crowell stepped forward. "Locklear's not your business. Never was. I'm that surprised he brought you this far. Your business is to move this wagon. We have come to help you." Crowell spoke slowly, evenly. "Suffolk is not far, only it's Tory now. We'll take you a safe way around to Liston's farm and the Chesapeake. Captain?"

Erskin's arm tightened around George's shoulders, signaling him to stay quiet. Then Erskin nodded to Crowell.

The mules strained. The wagon moved. The cargo was battened tight under oilskins. George took no pride in the wheels, turning smoothly in sockets he and John Farrow had fitted. He walked behind Erskin, his heart numb. He wore the moccasins Johnny had given him when he lost his boots. He wore the coat over his jacket, but it was still too big. He thought of the bullet smashing into the hood, shattering the glass-bead eyes.

Reeve led the mules. Crowell kicked along beside Erskin, telling him the latest news. George didn't care about Indian massacres in western Carolina and Virginia, about the new treaty between the Cherokees and King George III. When Loyalists and Cherokees joined along the western frontier, Crowell reported, the Great Appalachian Trail that ran from Pennsylvania to Georgia would be united behind the king. The Americans would be choke-squeezed between the mountains and the sea.

"You'd better tell about the lady," Reeve called back to Crowell. "You ought to tell them, Reuben."

George lost the answer in the gathering dark. It was sixteen long, roundabout miles to Morris Liston's land. He was staggering tired when the mules, scenting the home barn, plodded faster down a low hill. The farm might once have been an estate, a neat and prosperous expanse of alfalfa and tobacco, of grazing land for cows and sheep and racing thoroughbreds, of white fencing and a formal entrance drive for

Williamsburg carriages. George saw only one wing of what had been a large house and a barn.

George followed Erskin into the barn and sank wearily into a bed of straw. Crowell and Reeve unhitched the mules and fed them. Warily, Erskin kept his eye on the wagon, pulled inside the barn. George huddled miserably in Johnny's coat. At length, Erskin left the two guides outside the barn and walked back to his son. He knelt down.

"Campbell told me Locklear might be working for the Tories. He was only hired help, son. That's why I kept my distance. I didn't tell you. I didn't know for sure it was true."

"It wasn't true," George almost sobbed.

Erskin waited a moment. "There's nothing we can do about it. You were too easy, too anxious to be his friend. We'll trust no one from now on. Do you understand, son?"

George shuddered agreement.

"I'm going along to meet Liston. I'll bring you back some supper. Rest for a while."

"You are the boy I saw behind the wagon. Morris lied to me. Where is the boy, I asked, but Morris said there was no boy, only Captain Midgett and those miserable soldiers. It was Reuben Crowell who rode with you to the ship at South Quay. But you are here. You have come home."

Five minutes or five hours? George sat up, rubbing his eyes.

A middle-aged lady in a blue velvet cloak, lantern in hand, stood over him. She wore a white wig, making her pale face more ghostly in the flickering light. George stumbled to his feet, brushing straw from his clothes.

"Don't be afraid, young lad. You are in a democratic household, filled with liberty and happiness. Follow me."

George followed the lady from the barn to an arbor passageway, ceilinged with dead vines that swung lazily back and forth in the lantern light.

"We made our own wine from these grapes. Morris's grandfather brought cuttings from Bordeaux, in the south of France, after the Huguenots were condemned because they were Protestants in Catholic France. For that they were drawn and quartered, their intestines thrown to dogs, their heads cut off and put on spikes for all to see, all in the name of sweet Jesus Christ, Our Lord. The vines are dead now, just as the house and farm are dead, just as—"

"Sarah!"

A middle-aged gentleman ran through the double door at the end of the arbor. He was tall and thin, clad in blue velvet and a white silk shirt. He wore no wig. His natural white hair was pulled back into a ponytail and tied with a black velvet ribbon.

"Cayce!" he called.

"There *was* a boy, Morris. You lied to me."

"Cayce! For God's own sake!"

A black manservant came through the doorway and tenderly, with great care, led the woman inside.

"You are indeed a boy," the gentleman said hastily, taking George by the arm. "I am Morris Liston. I apologize for my wife. Mrs. Liston is not well. I am dining with your father. Please join us."

George wonderingly followed the gentleman through a foyer into a brightly lighted room with a dining table and chairs at one end and a desk and sitting area at the other. Erskin, looking gruff and deadpan, stood at the mantel of an open-hearth fire.

"Your son, sir," Morris Liston flustered. "I hope you are both hungry."

George took one look at Erskin and knew his thoughts. Morris Liston was a lace-handkerchief coward, a silver-snuffbox weakling. George knew the look well, because it had so often been directed at him.

"Locklear did his job," Erskin said. "Took us through the Dismal. You had him killed. You say my journey ends here. I say we are going to Pennsylvania. I am flummoxed."

"Dine now, talk later, Captain Midgett. You must not waste the table I have prepared for you."

George had never seen nor tasted such food: turtle soup with celery, onion, and carrot; roast chicken and country-fried steak; sweet yams and string beans; Sally Lunn cake and dark, rich coffee. The meal was served by the black man who had led Sarah Liston away.

George took a second serving of the light pound cake as Erskin and Liston moved to the hearth. Liston poured glasses of port and offered Erskin a rack of pipes with long stems and a jar of tobacco.

"This is Barbadian tobacco, flavored with nectar of orange.

Far better, I fear, than our Virginia burley. Now, about those supplies."

"Why did you have Locklear killed?" Erskin asked.

"I did not have him killed, sir. Reuben and Mathew kill any Indian they can find. They are cousins, all that is left of an entire family of forty-seven people. The family was staking a land grant to the west. Reuben and Mathew were away hunting. When they returned, they found only ashes and pieces of what had been living people. I offer no further explanation.

"Now, I believe that the future of our country lies in the West and that our natural enemies are Indians. By 'country,' Captain Midgett, I mean this great Commonwealth of Virginia. I would remind you, sir, that I hold first command in the Virginia Militia. I would also remind you that I was an alternate delegate to the Philadelphia Convention in 1776. I can assure you that General Washington once had my greatest confidence. As a fellow-Virginian, I could not say otherwise. But no longer. It was a foolish decision, to choose Valley Forge as winter quarters. The best military men say so. He is wide open to the British in Philadelphia, as well as to Indians in the Wyoming Valley, in northern Pennsylvania. He has put his soldiers into a hopeless trap. I am told they are deserting by the hundreds.

"Virginia, however, can still be defended. Virginia can be saved. But I badly need your supplies. We are stocking local garrisons in the Suffolk area. Other men under my command are doing the same in their districts."

Erskin swore. George knew that he wanted his own pipe and tobacco and a chair he could safely sit in. The obscenity made Morris Liston pull out a handkerchief and cough into it.

"Virginia is not my country," Erskin announced. "Ocracoke Island is my country. The boy here is my army. George, tell the colonel about old Hannah."

"It was the pigs," George began, "our meat for the winter." Then he told the story of Hannah O'Neal and the common-consent verdict of the village of Ocracoke.

Colonel Liston spent several moments with his handkerchief before he spoke. "Why, surely, I understand. You would certainly want to even the score. It is right and just that you do this." His mood seemed feverish as he moved to the desk, opened a locked drawer, and took out a large chart. He unrolled the chart on the dining table and flattened it with two candelabra. "If only it were possible. See here, outside Suffolk. And here is the route Campbell used six months ago. Overland. From South Quay through Virginia into Maryland to Pennsylvania. All that is changed now. Campbell should have warned you."

Liston's voice turned high and shrill. George studied the map carefully. He looked to his father.

"But there is another route," George said. "Straight up the Chesapeake to the Delaware to Marcus Hook—"

"The Chesapeake? You would be blown out of the water. You would not get ten miles beyond Smith Island."

George dared not look at his father. Had Liston betrayed them? The Chesapeake was where they were supposed to go, all the way up the Chesapeake.

94

"Captain Midgett." Morris Liston paced himself carefully. "My house was burned when I was away to Philadelphia. My son—but I will not speak of my son. Know only that I know more about this war, and these times, than you do. Venture into the bay and you will lose everything. Your lives first of all."

George didn't see Sarah Liston run at him from behind. He only felt the talon grip of her hands.

Both Erskin and Liston moved toward George, but stopped, held back by something George could not see.

Morris Liston spoke to George with a voice and look of awful pain. "We lost our boy. Just your age. Perhaps you would sleep in his room tonight. A favor to me, young sir."

George shivered as the hold on him tightened.

"You would take my son hostage?" Erskin bellowed.

"Do not slander me," Liston replied. "A few hours only. Cayce—take care of him."

While Erskin stood by, unable to attack a crazy woman, the black manservant lifted George by his elbows and carried him into the strangest night of his life.

He was stripped of his clothes and put into a tin tub filled with hot water. He was scrubbed until every inch of his body burned and glistened clean. Cayce washed his hair, poured lemon-scented rinse water over his hair and body, rubbed and wrapped him dry in a large towel. Dressed in a linen nightshirt that fell below his knees, slippered in bright-red velvet shoes embroidered with gold lions, he was carried down a hall to a bedroom and Sarah Liston, waiting beside a four-poster bed. The covers were pulled back, the pillows puffed. He was tucked into the bed for what might be forever. He watched, terrified, as Cayce disappeared.

The garbled madness that poured out of Sarah Liston reminded George of shipwreck fever. He sympathized, for he understood the sad loneliness of people who had lost everything and were lost themselves. Sometimes she thought he was George. Then, midsentence, he was her son.

"He was our only child. Our Peter. Oh, Peter. I married Morris out of Charleston, out of my uncle's house on Tradd Street. It was a year later Peter was born.

"Always we planned his schooling. He was two years old when Morris and I went to London and enrolled him at Temple Court. I had been educated in Paris. Morris had his degree in London, at Gray's Inn at Temple Court, where the great Francis Bacon wrote his essays and plays, where his father and grandfather had lived and studied.

"Peter had the best tutors in Virginia. The farm was not as it is now. This farm was a kingdom. Guests came from Williamsburg and Charlottesville, from Boston and New York, and stayed for months. Peter met everyone. He spoke both French and German by the time he was nine years old.

"It happened—why did it happen—that Peter—he was only twelve years old—sailed for London at the time of the riot in Boston. He sailed out of Wilmington. His ship was captured, taken as an example. We heard nothing about it for months. We thought he was safe. But no. Months later we knew that all the men and boys were put on a British warship and taken to Barbados in the Caribbean.

"The trouble in Boston made the British brutes. They'd

always been our friends. They took our children. My son, all the boys, were only students. What did they know of rebellion? All were taken to Barbados and left in rotting prison ships.

"My husband was responsible for our son's death. I knew nothing of his politics, his treason against England. I never knew that his business affairs in Williamsburg and Philadelphia involved treason. I never knew that John Randolph and Thomas Jefferson, our dear friends, would stoop to treason.

"They seduced Morris with their ideas. Peter was dead, gone forever, and I never knew why. But I began to know when Morris went to that Convention in Philadelphia, as an alternate delegate. Then only God knew my heart. Morris had betrayed his own son by his treason long before he sailed.

"I was with friends in Williamsburg while Morris was in Philadelphia. Our house was burned, everything stolen. Didn't he know that the loyal people in Suffolk would do that? Ah, but he has suffered his own hell.

"He thought the Declaration of Independence only a warning, only a signal to the king that we wanted fairness. Only a warning! How many husbands and brothers and sons has it killed?

"Morris never speaks of it now, the Declaration of Independence—this thing he would have signed had it been necessary. But Virginia had so many traitors he wasn't needed."

"I am sorry about Peter," George murmured, going in and out of sleep.

The name of Peter sent her deeper into chaos. She brought George wide awake with hurtful hands.

"Why, Peter, you have come home, and I must know everything. I haven't seen a *London Times* for months. Did you see David Garrick on the London stage? Did you take a holiday in Paris? Young Mozart is there for the winter. He is a genius, they say, and his mother a charmer. Did you go to Italy? I must know everything, Peter. Did you bring me new books? Did you bring your father a new wig? Did you . . ."

When did the candle sputter and darkness lull her quiet? George never knew. He thought he had slept only a few minutes when Cayce wakened him in the dark with hot tea, bread, and bacon.

"You must hurry," Cayce whispered. "Don't make a sound. Your father has gone ahead with the soldiers. I will show you where to go."

George jerked into his clothes and Johnny's coat. He reached for his moccasins.

Cayce held out boots, beautiful English leather boots. George hesitated.

"Don't waste time."

George pulled on the dead boy's boots. They fit.

Cayce went through the window first and held out his arms. George jumped. Together they ran through the dark until George heard the wagon wheels. Cayce waved him on. Everything moved at top speed. Crowell was beating the mules. Erskin was running beside Reeve. George caught up, fell behind, caught up again. Erskin looked back, saw he was there, beckoned him to his side with a smile of relief. Dirt ran into beach sand. George heard the cry of whistling swans.

"You won't get there," Reeve whined, unhitching the mules. "It's all thrown to the devil's pot."

"Shut up, Mathew," Crowell hissed.

The wheels were off the wagon and stowed. Erskin and Crowell launched the barge into Chesapeake Bay. George splashed through the shallows, christening his fine new boots, and climbed aboard. Erskin raised the sail.

Crowell had a last word. "Don't think badly of our colonel, Midgett. He lost his nerve is all. Godspeed."

The sail took the wind. The barge creaked and moved. George took a farewell look. The mules, ears raised, mouths wide open, seemed to be laughing at him.

9

Erskin told him to keep moving. Erskin said the weather was no worse than weather at home. George felt the wind blowing stronger and the water chopping colder under a full-moon tide. He thought about walking to old Hannah's farm, his hands frozen to the slop buckets. He remembered Erskin with ice in his beard, head covered with frost. He knew what cold was, but not this cold.

It never ended: days and days of cold, with no escape into a warm house, no shelter from the wind. One gray morning after another, one gray afternoon after another, one solid-freeze night after another. Ice formed in the night and melted in daylight. Then it did not melt. Chunks of ice became islands of ice, as big as the barge itself.

Now and then George clasped the brass button in his pocket, remembering Hannah lying dead in the mud, seeing again the helpless anger on the faces of the villagers. He thought of how hard everyone had worked to build and load the barge. Each day that dawned with the barge still afloat and the cargo intact was a victory. Five weeks, Colonel Campbell had estimated their journey, five or six weeks. But time itself was frozen on the winter-locked Chesapeake.

The sail was useless. The barge crawled along the shore-line, both Erskin and George hacking and pushing with the poles. Pelicans and seagulls, stranded on the ice, searched for food that wasn't there. Smaller birds, their wings broken in the wind, lay dying around the barge. Overhead, wailing and screeching in instinctive triumph, swans and geese flew south.

Erskin's pole slipped. George almost screamed when the backlash slush hit his face. The barge snagged on a sandbar under the slush and froze.

"Give me the towline," Erskin said. "I will pull us free."

Erskin lowered himself into the water. The line tightened between the mast and his shoulders, and the barge moved, only to beach like a confused whale on the shore. Erskin sank down on the sand, head between his legs. George thought he might have fainted.

A woman walked slowly out of the scrub pine and holly just beyond the beach. She was over six feel tall, with a bright red kerchief tied around short, straw-colored hair. She wore a fur jacket and pants and leather boots with brass bells around the top. She stopped in front of Erskin, turned to see George when he came scrambling from the barge.

"We got stuck in the ice," George blurted out. "My father— that's my father—pulled us off the bar, only we ran aground."

The woman's face was fair and lightly-freckled, her eyes a mean, skeptical blue. She looked from Erskin to George, from George to Erskin.

"He's Erskin Midgett," George stuttered. "And I'm George."

The woman leaned down into Erskin's face and laughed, a gut-busting laugh. "I've heard of the Midgett men but never seen one. Are you alive, Midgett?"

Erskin raised his dark cloud of a face and rose to his feet. He was only a scant inch taller than the woman. His face grew darker.

Still laughing, the woman jumped on the barge and saw everything. It was as though she knew what to look for.

"God does love to make a fool and name him Midgett," the woman said when she returned. "Where are you going with that salt?"

Erskin swore.

The woman swore back.

Then George saw the look between them, a stalemate of admiration and something more.

"You would be from Kinnakeet or Chicamacomico, only places wild enough to hatch Midgetts," the woman said.

"We are traders going north," Erskin said.

"Monkey's foot and monkey's tail." The woman laughed and whistled. Four men appeared, as she had, from the scrub and moved between Erskin and the barge.

"I am Mackey Smith," the woman said. "And these are my friends and partners—Tack Bobby, Robin Burleigh, Ransom Smith, no relation, and Only Luke. Luke won't say his last name, so we call him Only for spite. This is Smith Island, as if you didn't know. We have watched you for two days, wanted you to keep coming our way. But for the weather, two British longboats would have had you for certain. You'd be eating roaches in a Maryland jail. Instead, you can eat pig with us."

"Thank you," Erskin said calmly. "We're hungry. Especially the boy."

George had seen men like this in Portsmouth: sharp and ragged, no waste timber on their bodies, no kindness in their eyes.

"Come along with me," Mackey said. "You'd do well, Midgett, to think of the boy."

Erskin turned away, put his hand on George's shoulder. George, tired and so cold, fell into step beside him. They walked to the top of a low hill, the highest point on the island, and Mackey Smith's house, a rambling hodgepodge of brick, wood, and tabby, a cementlike mix of sand and oyster shells. Mackey opened the one door and led them inside to a long, cedar-beamed room. One end was a junkyard of captain's chests, broken furniture, and fishing gear. The other end was home.

George almost wept when he saw the fire, the roasting pig, the steaming kettle. He ran to the hearth and warmed his hands.

"We have been cold," Erskin said.

"Nor'easter blowing in," Mackey said. "Can't nobody go nowhere. Not even you, Midgett. Take off your coats and dry them. Boots, too. There's privilege before hanging. Make yourselves to home." She laughed again, her eyes the same mean, skeptical blue.

Erskin took out his pipe, lit it with a taper from the fire. George wondered why it took so long. Erskin lit his pipe a dozen times a day. Now he turned the taper back and forth, waiting for the flame to settle. At last fragrant smoke trailed from his nostrils. Not once did he move his head or turn his gaze from Mackey Smith's face.

"I will have a rum, then," Erskin said. "The boy as well."

The last thing George remembered was the taste of the rum in the silver goblet, warm and smooth and laced with honey. Released from the tight heaviness of wet boots and Johnny's coat, he stretched beside the fire to watch the war between Erskin and Mackey, to listen to the noise of winter outside the door, and to drift, finally, into exhausted sleep.

When he wakened, Erskin and Mackey were nowhere to be seen. The four friends and partners were sitting in front of the hearth eating pig and corn pudding.

"Where is my father?" George asked.

"In the back room with Mackey," Robin Burleigh said.

"I would say you just lost ten guineas," Tack Bobby said, flipping an hourglass on the floor beside him.

"Only said half an hour, not me," Robin said.

"That was two hours ago Only said that. He's out. I will put twenty guineas on the next hour."

"He is either a dead man by now," Ransom said, "or we have all lost two hundred pounds of salt."

"Fair is fair," Only said. "Honor among thieves."

"Where is my father?" George repeated.

Ransom Smith gave a loud bellow and yanked George into the circle. "Your father, lad, and our Mackey are working out the negotiations by which we will all agree to proceed one way or the other—which means that I think you had better shut up. Have some pig and pudding."

"Are you a pirate?" George asked, sucking roast pig drippings from his fingers.

"We're a lot of things," Only Luke answered. "Same as you. We're not priests, I'll admit. We don't rob the rich and give to the poor. We rob the rich and give to ourselves, same as merchants and bankers."

"One question shuts the door," Ransom said darkly. "The second locks it. That means mind your own business." He looked beyond them. "We just lost the salt."

Mackey sailed into the room on bare feet, whirling around in a long, bright-red dress. She kicked at the boys playfully, including George, and passed around dusty wine bottles she carried in each hand. Erskin had washed and shaved. He, too, was barefooted and wore a white silk shirt. Smiling to himself, Erskin clapped George on the back and shot him a conspiratorial wink. George almost fell off the hearth. His smile broadening, Erskin took a plate to the steaming pots and helped himself to a large meal. Whooping, hollering, the boys drew a large chest to the center of the room, opened it, and drew out a glittering array of silk shirts, scarves, petticoats, and yards of ribbon.

The storm and the party lasted for three days. Outside, snow and sleet thick-sealed the house with ice.

Inside, everyone ate pig and pulled roasted oysters and clams from the fire. Only Luke made a stew from the leftovers and everyone ate that. Rum and wine washed down corn pudding and cake. As Tack Bobby said, "Sometimes we got nothing to eat, but we have plenty of fine wine to wash down the nothing." George ate and drank himself into several deep snores.

Everyone danced when Tack Bobby played his pipes. All the men, even Erskin, danced for Mackey; then Mackey danced for the men. George tried to imitate Only Luke's flip twirls and almost broke his nose. Tack Bobby played his pipes and danced at the same time, and Robin told George that was an accomplishment.

Everyone talked.

Ransom Smith had worked on a slaver from Liverpool to East Guinea to Barbados. He had sailed in the Greek islands and had spent a day and a night in Athens.

Tack Bobby had been bonded to Captain James Cook as cabin boy on his first voyage to the South Seas. Cook was out there again, Bobby had heard, on his third voyage.

Robin Burleigh had never gone beyond the bay.

Only Luke was a Welshman, drummed out of the king's service for thieving, gambling, whoring, drunkenness, and gouging. He had jumped ship in Baltimore five years earlier. There was more, but it was nobody's business.

Mackey had been born on Smith Island. Orphaned at 15, she stayed on in her grandfather's house. She always had friends and partners. She always managed for herself because the Good Lord had made her big and strong. If she had been puny, she would have gone into the High Church convent at Chestertown. She planned to be married there— if and when.

On the third morning, Mackey threw the door open to fresh air and brilliant light. The men washed and shaved themselves sober and got down to business.

"We would speak to you about the barge, Erskin," Mackey said. "Are you still wanting to go north?"

Erskin nodded. "We are beholden to our village, Mackey."

"I'd do it just to do it," Only said.

"You wouldn't be doing it," Ransom said. "It's Erskin and George will be blown out of the water."

"Get out the charts," Mackey said at last. "I'd have Erskin look at the odds."

Mackey and the boys knew every inch of every mile, every cove and inlet on the bay. Robin knew where they could put in at night and safely light the sand fire. Only knew every sandbar and riptide current. Ransom searched through the junkyard heap and found hooks to fit on the end of the poles—six-inch iron claws. He also gave George a rusty ice axe and set him to work cleaning it.

They spent hours considering what might happen. The worst thing would be actual boarding, search, and seizure. If the British found the salt, they were dead fish in a dead sea. The flags, Mackey said, were an absolutely last-resort measure.

"Oh, those flags," Only scoffed. "Mackey does love those flags."

"A barge is different from an oyster rig," Mackey said. "It's worth trying."

She opened the captain's chest. Now, instead of pulling out silks, she rummaged to the bottom and spilled out the flags. For over two hundred years, pirates had returned to Smith Island with stolen or surrendered flags. A Hapsburg coat of arms from Germany. A Venetian gold lion on a black field. Clan flags that had flown over Scottish fields. More than a dozen Union Jacks of all sizes.

"Well, that just won't work," Only again protested. "Too close to home. The Brits are very sensitive about the Jack."

"I hope so." Mackey was determined. "It's not likely a barge on the bay would be Greek or Portuguese. Why not the Jack? Never underestimate British pride and arrogance."

"What's this?" George picked up a small square.

"American," Mackey replied. "Stars and stripes. Made by a captured sailor on a prison ship. Tell how we got it, Robin."

George carefully examined the small square, not much larger than his hand. The background was red twill, fabric from an officer's coat. The stripes were thin strips of white silk. The stars were a simple cross-stitch of yellow thread.

"It was in a letter," Robin answered. "Poor son of a bitch put it in a letter to his family. We thought we stole a wages bag, and it was mail."

"Can I have it?" George asked Mackey.

"Why not? It's our flag, I guess, if we want to fly a flag. We live free and independent on Smith Island. Always have. But I don't mind calling myself an American."

"Me neither," Tack Bobby said. "Because the Americans

will win. Not this year. Not maybe in five years. But we'll win. The land is too big. Nobody can control it except the people who live here. The British will get tired and go home, where they should've stayed in the first place."

"The long rifle will win the war," Ransom Smith said. He opened another chest and brought out a long object wrapped in a piece of Oriental carpeting. He unrolled the carpet carefully, almost lovingly. "Took me a year to find one of these to steal." The long, gray-blue barrel projecting from the polished wooden stock looked out of proportion. Ransom put it to his shoulder and sighted an imaginary target.

"There's never been a rifle like this, not in Europe, not anywhere. Funny thing, how weapons get invented during peacetime. Frontiersmen needed a rifle that would shoot long. A German locksmith in Philadelphia came up with this. Worked on it for years. He stretched out the barrel and rifled it narrow inside, like a long screw with a very fine thread. This thing will put a bullet dead center at six-hundred yards. Frontiersmen can pick off squirrels and small game they can hardly see. If you can center a squirrel at six-hundred yards, what can you do to a man?

"This rifle is changing the way men fight. The British move in lines—up, shoot, fall back, second line up, shoot, fall back. The Americans, especially the southards, like to shoot get Americans to stand still in a line. Soon's we get enough from cover, like they're shooting game. Why, nobody can of these long rifles, the British will go home."

"The warships in the bay aren't squirrels," Mackey said.

She turned to Erskin and George. "We've showed you all we know. Tack Bobby can keep an eye on you for a few days, but that's about it."

"I would thank all of you for the both of us," Erskin said rather formally. He turned to George. "It's time to go, son."

George had the new charts in his head, a large Union Jack tied to a pole, and the small American flag in the pocket of Johnny's beaver coat. The boys sailed the barge out of the hideaway bay to Mackey's dock, cargo and gear in order. The pantry chest was stocked with fresh bread, jerky, and whale oil.

Tack Bobby and Only hoisted George on their shoulders and plunked him aboard the barge, giving him last-minute advice about women and how to avoid marriage. George took the banter in stride until he saw Erskin take Mackey in his arms for a long moment.

And we weren't supposed to trust anyone, George thought wryly. To his astonishment, Erskin and Mackey broke apart with unabashed, ringing laughter. One leap put Erskin at George's side.

Within minutes, the shore and scrub pine of Smith Island, and all that had happened there, were veiled in thick fog.

"At first I thought they would kill us," George said, somewhat testily. "But they didn't."

"Only woman I ever knew," Erskin replied, "who wasn't skittish."

10

The captain's spyglass moved right and left, came to rest. George imagined the view: a barge low in the water, a barge so loaded with contraband it couldn't move out of the way. The warship was so close that George could see the British monkeys—sailors in pea jackets and white neckerchiefs— climbing up and down the lines. The ship's whistles blew.

Deafened and angry, because Erskin pretended the ship wasn't there, the two patrol boats weren't there, nothing was there but his own purpose, George crawled up on the salt barrels and raised the pole.

The Union Jack flew over the barge. George waved it in full view of the captain's glass. He waved and smiled and smiled and waved.

The ship veered left, its wake crashing against the barge so violently George was knocked to his knees. He was up again in an instant, waving the Jack and smiling.

Erskin thought it was funny, how easily the British were fooled. George didn't think it was funny after the nineteenth time. When the frostbitten land of Aberdeen came into view, he didn't think anything was funny. He couldn't eat. He was hot and cold at the same time. He dreaded the moment when Erskin would see his sickness.

The barge docked; the towline was fastened to a tree on the deserted end of Turkey Point. Erskin was gone all day, looking for a man named John Darby. When he returned, George was huddled under blankets, shivering and burning.

"Son." Erskin touched his forehead, tried to warm his hands. "We're here, on the peninsula at Turkey Point. I found Darby. What's wrong?"

"I don't know," George whispered.

Erskin watched him through the night, keeping the sand fire burning. But there was more light than heat from the fire.

"It's my cousin Silas who'll stop you," John Darby announced when he arrived the next morning. He led four mules, who looked as out of joint as their owner. "You can take the mules and go overland, or I can cross you to the Delaware River, but Silas will stop you either way. I haven't seen him for nigh onto two years. He runs Marcus Hook: the wharf, the Darby Inn. A merchant banker. He was always Tory, and he's grown in importance. Your boy looks peaked. I tell you this for his sake. Things have changed since my contract with Colonel Campbell. Half the men at Valley Forge are gone—deserted or dead. Over half."

"Darby," Erskin said, "how many cousins do you have?"

"Everyone's Darby hereabouts, Darby or Dumfries. Every one a turncoat. I risked my life to meet you, Midgett." He was a small, dark-faced man who stood first on his right leg, then his left. "I'd go back, to Baltimore or somewheres south."

"My boy will die if I go back. How far overland to the Delaware?"

"One day, maybe two."

"Up the Delaware to Marcus Hook?"

"One day, maybe half a day with the wind."

"We will move then."

"You can't, Midgett. I'm killed if I don't turn you back."

"You're killed if you don't help me move. You're killed if I find out you're not true. The boy and I have been pulled every which way. Every day a mystery. More miles of cold, cowardice, and stupidity. I am tired of Tory talk, and Indian talk, and rebel talk, and all talk. I am tired of opinionation. My boy is sick, and you will help me fix the wheels and hitch the mules, and we will move."

The wagon moved, over the rough terrain of Elk Neck Forest, over the pine-needled land that joined the great Chesapeake to the great Delaware. George felt the wagon turn back into a barge, smelled salt water, and heard the cry of gulls.

George wandered aimless in dreams. Jenny Scarborough had just baked a spice cake. Grizelle wore a locket with a green ribbon. Hannah O'Neal showed him a litter of new shoats. Erskin swore at him. The villagers laughed at him.

He was no longer cold. He threw off the blankets and his clothes. He was naked and blazing. Hard hands pushed him

113

back to the oven. Hard hands held his mouth open, filled it with laudanum, the dream medicine that killed pain. The opiate wore off. Another spasm, another dry heave that clotted red spittle on his teeth and lips. Hard hands bound his feet and hands still.

The barge moved steady up the Delaware to Marcus Hook, dodging chunks of ice.

"Barge coming in!" a boy cried from the wharf.

Erskin took his time, threw the line to the boy, asked for the harbor master, lit his pipe. Horsemen in red and green jackets rode dockside. Wagons, carts, carriages echoed along a maze of dirt paths and cobbled streets.

Silas Darby also took his time, strolling from his office, followed by a band of sailors, clerks, and shrill women—the wharf-rat population of a backwater seaport.

"Silas Darby." Erskin rose to his full height. "I am Erskin Midgett, sir, and I ask your permission to anchor here and come dockside."

Silas Darby stood commanding and cold in front of his followers. "State your business in Marcus Hook, sir."

"My son is sick with fever and half-dead. I need a doctor."

Silas Darby walked from one end of the barge to the other. Erskin threw off the oilskins, hiding nothing. Only George, huddled in blankets, could not be seen. Silas Darby picked up the pole with the Union Jack, tossed it aside with an ugly laugh.

"Come now, Captain Midgett. I am not blind nor dumb after two years of war. The deer- and bearskins might make you an Indian trader, although I doubt it. Where are you bound with so much salt? Salt is the lifeblood of an army. Are you a rebel, sir? Is Marcus Hook your last way station to Valley Forge and the American army?"

Erskin shrugged, puffed calmly on his pipe. "My son is my business here. Besides, I am told there is a British army roundabout Philadelphia. It's true I am a trader. It's also true that salt is gold anywhere."

"How many pounds?"

"Two hundred."

Darby whistled, forgetting his importance in the weight and wonder of so much salt.

"It is honest salt, sir," Erskin said, "as honest as the bread it will flavor. Purchased and passed by the harbor master at Portsmouth, down in Tory Carolina."

"God save the king!" Darby's entourage set up a cry.

"God bless him forever!"

"Dumfries District, Darby Town,

"O Lord in mercy do look down!

"The land is poor, the people too,

"If they don't steal, what will they do?"

Darby turned to silence the crowd. At that moment, two horsemen in scarlet jackets dismounted and boarded the barge. The first officer picked up the flagpole and set it against the mast. The officers obviously annoyed Darby.

"No man's allegiance is believed," he muttered. "These goons follow me everywhere. Where is the sick boy?"

Erskin folded the blanket away from George's face. He lifted him in his arms.

Darby stepped back. "We have no pox here. I am responsible for the health of my citizens."

"It is not pox, Silas, but fever. I will take the boy home.
I will send for Dr. Lindsay."

Silas Darby turned, startled. "Margaret, I have asked you
not to come here."

"I brought your lunch."

The woman who stepped from the carriage wore a long,
black wool cloak and black shawl and carried a basket. She
was a small woman with a tired face. Her voice, quiet and
low, was louder than the buzz of anger, surprise, and curiosity.

"You will go home, Margaret."

"I will go where I please, Silas. Bring the boy to me. Put
him in the carriage."

George did not know barge from wagon from carriage. He
did not know that he was still alive. But the woman's voice
was so soft, so sweet and gentle, that at last he wanted to
see her face.

"Not Jenny. I am not Jenny. I am Margaret. Can you hear
me?"

She was a young woman without the cape and shawl. She
looked pleased and happy.

He was in Marcus Hook, wherever that was. He was get-
ting well. Yes, he wanted more soup. Yes, he was George
Midgett, and where was his father?

"He sat on the barge for two days. He had a riverman's
pole, tipped with an iron claw, suitable for peeling off a
man's face or stirring his entrails. My Silas is a hard man,
but he is not a murderer. He offered a business deal. Your

116

father could have food and lodging at the inn until you are well. Silas would fix the wheels on the barge and keep it in the courtyard behind the inn. They have not yet reached a trade agreement. Silas wants that salt very badly. It is months since so much salt has been offered for sale. Perhaps, now you have sense again, you will tell me the truth about it."

"The truth?" George sat up.

"Never mind. I shall miss the terror of your father's impatience. I never saw such a man. He doesn't understand sickness, the slowness of nature's healing. He doesn't appreciate the skill of a doctor trained in Edinburgh and the care of a woman who raised six young brothers and sisters. I confess you were back and forth many times. Fevered and thrashing and drowning."

The blur of journey, the time until now, straightened out in George's mind. Marcus Hook. Only seventeen miles to go ... Seventeen miles. He turned to Margaret Darby, who was standing by the window, looking out at the town square.

"Where did you come from?" she asked. "Where were you going?"

George didn't answer.

"I have seen everything in the square," Margaret said quietly. "I have seen hangings and whippings and brandings. Some were thieves and gougers, deserving punishment. Some were common tarts, too quick and easy with the bodies God designed. One was a parson who preached free will. But most were political prisoners. Patriot and Loyalist alike have been tortured in the square, sentenced by the day's news. A week ago, a boy your age was whipped half to death because he was starving. He was a deserter, stealing bread and jerky to see him home. It's not the cold that's killing Washington's men. It's hunger.

"Where were you going?" she asked again.

There came the slam of a door, the thunk of boots, then the abrupt and powerful blast of Erskin's presence. Once inside the room, however, confronted by the small woman and his son, he seemed to shrink, to grow bewildered and puzzled.

Startled, George saw how Erskin had changed. A pallor underneath his red scraggle beard cast dark shadows of worry across his face. His once giant shoulders had an old man's hunch and sag. What had Silas Darby done to him? Or what, George thought achingly, have I and my weakness done to him?

"You know me, then," Erskin said gently. "This is the first day you have known me."

"George is himself again," Margaret said, moving a chair beside the bed. "Please sit down. I can see you have made a decision."

"Almost." Erskin ignored the chair. "I am about to sell my cargo to your husband. He will move the wagon and supplies into the dockside warehouse this afternoon. I have to take my boy home when he can travel. I have no other choice."

Erskin did not return George's look.

"I will get one hundred guineas for the salt. Twenty for the hides. Sixteen for the laudanum and miscellaneous. It is fair. Silas will give me gold coin and two horses. We will go home overland through Maryland."

"Everything?" George asked. "The sweaters? The pipes and tobacco?"

"I said everything."

"It is my fault." George tried to hold back tears. "I got fever and it is my fault."

"It is a business decision. Get dressed."

"It is my fault," George repeated in a daze.

"Stop sniveling!"

"It is nobody's fault." Margaret moved to the bed to soothe George. "My husband beat your father down. It is not the first time he has served both king and purse." She looked at Erskin. "So your story was true, all that nonsense about being a commercial trader."

Erskin, fierce and angry, glared at her. "Get the boy's clothes."

"You have been outwitted, outtraded, and worn down."

"A mule doesn't care who owns him." Erskin choked out the words. "It is the same harness and plow. So it is with my cargo. We can go under guard to Philadelphia, with Silas taking the profit. Or he can take the profit here and let us go home. Don't you think I know your husband's authority?"

"We were going to the camp," George said. "To Valley Forge."

George's voice rose over Erskin's protest. He told Margaret about Hannah and the pigs, about the raiding party, about the common consent of the villagers.

Yet Margaret seemed not to hear. She moved again to the window and the view of the square. "It was December seventeenth the army came, camping around an iron forge the valley farmers used for plowshares and shoeing horses and mules. Eleven thousand men, signed up for one and two years. Some were only boys sold to a war instead of a workhouse. Some were veterans from as far back as Lexington. Others were nobodies—strays and ruffians—the kind who follow the beat of any drum. Eleven thousand men.

"The weather went bad after Christmas, the worst I've seen since childhood. Still the wagons went through Marcus Hook. Silas was beside himself. He hadn't the force to stop them. The weather stopped the supplies. Snow and ice—like now. Silas took heart when the deserters started coming through. First the one- and two-year men. Then the ones signed up for the duration of the war. Only four thousand left now, perhaps fewer."

Her voice changed, grew strong in purpose. "But it is four thousand. Even if it were three or two, Washington would stick and stay stubborn, keep them drilling and battle sharp. Spring is sooner every hour.

"Everything counts. The smallest things. Every peck of potatoes, every pound of flour, every piece of leather, and yard of cloth. Two hundred pounds of salt is a miracle. Besides preserving, besides bread and porridge and the simple joy of taste, they can use it for barter with Tory farmers."

"It's too late now," Erskin muttered. "I am to take the money this afternoon. I would thank you now for the boy's life."

"There are two more lives," Margaret said quietly. "I have two brothers at the camp."

Erskin's face grew darker. His eyes, flat and leaden, searched the floor.

"They were the most trouble to raise," Margaret said. "Always into trouble, high-spirited and rebellious. There were seven of us, four boys and three girls. Since I was the first, I raised them up when our mother died. I saw them all away from home, saw my father to his place beside my mother, saw Silas at the funeral, knew he'd waited long enough. He did wait for me, and that's a reason for loving him, if no other. We never talk about my brothers. It is sometimes more than my heart can bear.

"Salt never killed anyone. There are no muskets or powder in your cargo. If you and George will do as I say, you will be guilty only of mercy."

George started up with a thrill of hope. Only 17 miles.

"Get the money and horses from Silas," Margaret said. "Leave Marcus Hook this afternoon. Wait outside town until eight o'clock. You will hear the church bell. Bring the horses to the warehouse. I will be there."

"You are crazy," Erskin said with his hard laugh. "What about the guard? Silas will put an armed guard around the warehouse."

"They are old duffers. I know them. I also know Silas. He will be at the inn planning Saturday's auction."

"The guard will not be fooled?" Erskin asked incredulously.

"Money will talk to them."

"What money?"

"The money Silas gives you this afternoon. You will sell your cargo and buy it back."

"You are crazy," Erskin repeated. "You are his wife."

"I had brothers before I had a husband."

Erskin swore, but under his breath. "Silas will not be foxed. He will know the guard was bribed. He will know who did it."

"What will he know?" For a small woman, Margaret Darby could loom large. "That his lifelong belief in money is justified? That other men like to stuff their pockets? Will he go about town saying that he was flummoxed by a woman and that woman his wife? What will he know?"

"There is more to it than that," Erskin said. "Silas will be after us tomorrow morning with half this Tory town."

"Are you afraid, Captain Midgett? Isn't morning years away? Won't you be at Valley Forge if you drive through the night?"

"We'll be there," George declared, already out of the bed and pulling on his boots, reaching for Johnny's coat. "It's a straight road north. I know the way."

Erskin, outnumbered, smiled gravely. "You women are the real soldiers," he said to Margaret Darby, then turned to George. "You are still sick. I'm going back to the inn and take the man's money. You are sick until Margaret tells you otherwise."

George always remembered the sound of the church bell as he and Margaret ran through the night streets. There were only two guards at the warehouse, ale-sodden and cursing the cold. Margaret shared her cloak with George, quiet and out of sight, as Erskin appeared from the dockside direction. Then the muffled exchange of the king's silver and gold coin for the warehouse keys. A few moments more, and the guards were gone.

He remembered the glow of Margaret's lamp as Erskin hitched the two horses to the wagon and calmly, slowly, checked the wagon's cargo. Erskin sat at the front, flicked the reins. Margaret held the lantern high until they had cleared the warehouse door, her face strangely triumphant against her dark cloak.

At just after nine o'clock, the wagon moved on.

11

"Old wheezers," Erskin raged. "Broke down old wheezers."

Erskin drove through the night, cursing Silas Darby. At first light, George saw the trick Darby had played on them. The horses, brushed sleek and bloated with feed the afternoon before, were old wheezer farm animals, used-up windbags that were almost blind.

"What do I know about horses?" Erskin raged.

He jumped from the front of the wagon to lead the horses on foot. George stayed in the back, watching the red, pink, yellow light come over the horizon.

"What do you see?" Erskin called.

"Nothing."

The morning was snow-covered and bleak, an endless white expanse. The road was a straight dark slash through the snow, a mire of slush and deep ruts. Soon the hard crust that had formed during the night would melt, suck the wheels deeper.

"There is a field yonder to the left," Erskin said.

George cut chunks of bread and cold bacon for breakfast.

"How far now?" Erskin asked.

"I don't know."

"It's an old field or an orchard," Erskin said. "Look, the road winds to the right, then back to the left, curving around private land, I guess. We can take a shortcut through that field and pick up this road again yonder. I can see it. Save a mile, maybe more."

George didn't want to leave the main road, bad as it was. There was a big difference between an old field and an orchard. An old field was land that had been planted and harvested so many times the topsoil was worn out. Some old fields were flat and hard enough for horse racing. But orchard land was filled with tree stumps and holes.

"Shouldn't we stay on the main road?" George asked. "If it's private land?"

"We have been driving hard all night. These horses can't drive hard all morning. The camp can't be that far. We'll risk the field."

Erskin climbed down from the wagon, pipe in his mouth. Erskin didn't know horses. He didn't know fields. He was fussed and angry.

"You'll drive now," Erskin announced. "I'll walk ahead and test the ground."

George still hesitated.

"You want to keep fighting that foot-deep mud?"

The horses liked the fresh, unbroken snow. They moved faster.

George kept the reins tight. Erskin plunged directly ahead, his boots crunching a new path. Although trees on either side were iced to the breaking point, the snow wasn't deep. The ground underneath was solid. The horses moved faster.

The rising sun brightened a snow-bright landscape, making depth and distance deceptive. The horses moved still faster as George felt the sudden downhill lurch. Erskin instinctively jumped out of the way as George pulled the reins tighter.

The horses were too fast. The wagon was too fast. George looked back to see Erskin trying to run on new snow, slipping and stumbling in the tracks the horses and wheels had made.

The wagon bounced up, came down, bounced up again. The reins cut George's hands as he was thrown forward between the horses. He grabbed frantically for the yoke joining the horses, felt his legs and feet swinging in air. He hung terrified between the horses.

The wagon stopped, lurched lopsided.

"George!" Erskin yelled. "A back wheel is stuck in a hole. . . ."

George, panting as deep and hard as the horses, eased to the ground. The wagon creaked and moved as Erskin lifted the wheel free. The wagon settled dead still on an even keel.

Erskin swore. He swore again, louder. George crawled under the horses and ran back to him. Erskin was lying face down behind the wagon, pushing himself up.

"That left wheel . . . it was the left wheel . . . it was cracked," Erskin said. "Is it out of the hole?"

"Yes. Only one spoke is cracked."

Erskin pushed up but didn't stand up. He rolled over to a sitting position and pulled his left leg straight. He slapped at the leg, straightened it with both hands. He looked surprised.

"The wheel rolled back over my leg. Couldn't stop it. I have broke my leg, I think."

Erskin leaned back on his elbows, lips pressed tight, chest moving up and down.

"Get the boot off, George. Get the boot off before it swells."

George unlaced the boot, propped Erskin's leg between his own legs, and pulled. The boot was wet and slick.

"If you are going to do it, do it."

George pulled the boot off. He gasped silently. A piece of Erskin's ankle bone was sticking through his wool sock.

Erskin lay back. His mouth relaxed. His chest rose and fell slowly.

"I have only broke my leg a little." Erskin looked pale and frightened and very surprised.

The white silence was deafening. Then George stuttered something and Erskin either murmured or groaned and neither heard what the other was saying. At length George scrambled into the wagon and mixed rum with one of the small bottles of laudanum. Erskin raised up to drink it down in one gulp, then reached in his jacket for his pipe and tobacco.

George fumbled with the flint against steel.

"I was never hurt before," Erskin said softly.

"It's not bad," George lied. He couldn't get a spark.

"I will do that. Feed the horses. No, not bad. I have only broke my leg a little."

The horses' heads nosed listless and tired in the feed bags. George kicked furiously at the treacherous snow. He could have helped Erskin lift the wheel. Why hadn't he waited?

Erskin smoked his pipe, asked for more rum. He settled, peaceful and still. George looked at his empty boot, standing upright. He remembered the cobbler's shop in Portsmouth and how Erskin had fussed at the price of new boots.

"Silas Darby would maybe have got us by now," Erskin said.

"Don't worry about Darby," George answered, almost abruptly. "We have to go back to where we cut off."

"We never went back before." Erskin pushed up in protest.

"It's not going back. We'll just cross over to the road again."

"We never went back before," Erskin repeated in a strange voice. Then George knew he wasn't thinking about the main road.

"I have been thinking all this long way about the boats,"— Erskin, relaxed again, spoke dreamily—"about going out in the boats in the storms. I would to God Moncie Scarborough was with me now. Moncie was a better man than Farrow. Farrow will go out, but he will wait a while. Farrow will wait for duty and honor to rise in him like yeast in cold flour. Then he will go out. Moncie would go at the first roar of the wind."

Erskin turned to George with a smile, his eyes filled with a sweet sadness that George had never seen before.

"But Moncie wasn't there, nor Farrow, nor anyone but me up to Kinnakeet. Nobody on Ocracoke was there.

"For two days we tried to get a boat out, me and the other scavengers. For two days we listened to the wind and the screaming. Two days that ship burned and finally drowned and we couldn't get a boat out.

"I was the only one still trying the third day, the morning you and Hannah washed up. I never saw such a storm, not even *The Polly Blue*—or such a morning after, calm and beautiful as Easter. I thought it was a keg or sack, or a sea chest, or anything but what it was. It was a sofa, out of a gentleman's cabin. Hannah was sitting on it, with you in her arms."

"Me and Hannah?" George asked, straining to hear.

Erskine nodded happily, as though the event had just occurred. "It was my line that pulled you in. You were my salvage. You were days old. Hannah was storm shocked and mostly drowned. I took you home."

"Me and Hannah?"

"Yes. I am telling you." Erskin's voice dropped to a confiding whisper. "I'd had a wife and baby, you know. I'd got my wife at fourteen, from Bath Town. Pretty girl. We were church married. It took us two years to get a baby. Then my son was born strangled and my wife died of childbed fever. I hadn't known sorrow until that day."

The laudanum, George decided, had put Erskin out of his head.

"Hannah didn't want to live," Erskin went on. "Maybe I did her no favor keeping her alive. Her hair turned white. Fever burned her flesh to bone, burned out her ears and tongue. But before she went speechless, she told me her name. And your name. You were Thomas Carey. Your parents were Irish folk with a king's grant for land in Carolina. You were born at sea, born too soon. Your mother died birthing you and your father drowned soon after, washed overboard while he was trying to lower a lifeboat.

"The storm took its pleasure that day. You were passed from the dead to the living. Then the living were only a few seamen and Hannah.

"Hannah never knew who put you in her arms, never knew how she came to be on that sofa the next morning." Erskin's voice filled with awe and wonder. "I have seen many things, but none stranger than the gift of you and Hannah. It was like God asking forgiveness for the storm."

Then Erskin's eyes snapped to the present moment, to the reality of George in front of him.

"I wanted a life again. I knew that Hannah would never hear or speak again. She couldn't read or write. How could she betray me? I got her well and left Kinnakeet, made a new life on Ocracoke. The villagers thought you were my own child."

"But I'm not?" George asked slowly, believing it at last. "I'm not your son?"

Erskin fisted his large hands, opened and closed them with an old anger. "You will not blame me now. You can-

130

not. I claimed you, named you after my father and grand-father, raised you and took care of you. How was I to find your people, your family, in Ireland? Maybe you had no other family, only your parents? How was I to know? You will not blame me now. You cannot."

George shook his head back and forth, trying not to cry.

"Hannah—" Erskin's resentment turned to sorrow and longing as he spoke the name—"Hannah always knew. I wanted her to accept you as my boy, just as everyone else did. But Hannah knew who you were, truly. That's why she let you help her on the farm. She knew your name was wrong. Always would be.

"It wasn't spite or meanness brought you on this journey, George. When Hannah was killed, I thought only that she had saved your life, and by saving your life had saved mine as well. We *both* owed Hannah. The villagers have nothing to do with it. It is our vengeance.

"I have been thinking about you all this long way. I know I have beat you down. I know I have been hard. I know I am not the father you might have had.

"But no matter what you think of me now, no matter how much you hate me or are afraid of me, you are my family, the only family I will ever have."

The world was so quiet. The world hadn't been so quiet since Erskin and George stood over Hannah O'Neal's grave.

George watched his shadow grow tall on the bright snow. He had never drowned in the nightmares. He had always waked up before going under for the last time. Like Jenny

131

and Moncie, like Burrus Wahab and Henry Frampton, he was a survivor. Now he understood their loneliness, their apartness, and their strength.

George climbed into the wagon and returned to Erskin with a pole.

"Use the pole as a crutch," George said. "I can't lift you. You have to get in the wagon. We have to move."

Erskin heaved into the wagon and lay face down. George turned him over, wrapped him in blankets, and pillowed his head on the sweaters the women of Ocracoke had made for the soldiers. Erskin closed his eyes.

George crawled to the front of the wagon, braced his knees, flicked the reins. The horses shuddered, tossed their heads, blew smoke, and turned back to the main road.

George talked to the horses. They didn't lame, didn't shy or balk as he eased them back into the foot-deep mud.

He drove on, looking up now and then to the sun moving toward noon. He wasn't so cold anymore. His boots, the boots that had belonged to Morris and Sarah Liston's lost boy, were dry and snug. Johnny's coat was warm—Johnny, the Croatan who had eaten raw fish, who was killed because he was an Indian. George fingered the button in the pocket of Johnny's coat, the brass button that Hannah had torn from her killer's jacket. George felt in the other pocket for the symbol of the war he knew nothing about, the small square of cross-stitched stars on white satin stripes against a red twill background.

"I don't mind calling myself an American," Mackey Smith had said, "as long as I stay free and independent."

George drove on, thinking about Ocracoke, especially about Jenny Scarborough. He hadn't realized how much he had missed Jenny. Behind her tough courage was kindness and love. Jenny had always looked after him, and Erskin as well. To think he had been too shy and clumsy to give Grizelle the locket with the green ribbon! His heart hurt when he remembered the sound of Grizelle's voice at the Christmas service.

George drove on and on, talking to the horses, keeping to the middle of the road, dodging the ruts on both sides. He saw farmhouses and red barns and two cows trying to graze under the snow.

Children wearing brightly colored caps and scarves appeared on the side of the road, laughing and waving. They wanted a ride on the wagon. George swore, threatening the children if they came closer. They only laughed and waved and made faces at him.

Other wagons rolled up behind him, passed him, splashed his face with mud. Drivers screamed at him to get out of the way, to get out of the middle of the road. George stayed where he was and talked to the horses.

Soldiers marched behind the wagon now. Cries went up around the wagon. The soldiers wanted a ride and rum, if he had any.

"Halt!"

The line of soldiers stopped.

"Stop and hold or I will fire! You in the wagon!"

Suddenly the reins were torn from George's hands. The horses and wagon jolted still. The soldier, the officer, was on a black horse as big as a mountain. George squinted up into the full fury of his eyes.

"Damn fool," the officer roared. "Didn't you hear me? You are holding up this line."

"Who are you?" George asked. His eyes hurt. He couldn't see with the sun in his eyes. Who was this man?

"Who am I? Why, by God, I am Samuel Downing, Second New Hampshire, and I am escorting these men. They are Greene's men, Nathaniel Greene, up from Kentucky, and they have been marching all night. Who the hell are you?"

George took a deep breath. "My name is Midgett, sir. George Midgett. This wagon is loaded with supplies for the army—the Americans. Two barrels of salt—"

"Salt?" Downing leaned forward in his saddle with a low whistle.

"Two hundred pounds of salt"—George nodded—"and hides and sweaters and medicine and tobacco. Erskin Midgett,"—George took another deep breath—"my father, is hurt bad. My father—"

But Downing was already off his horse and climbing into the wagon. He leaned over Erskin, drugged unconscious by the laudanum. Downing lifted the blankets.

"It's his left leg and ankle," George said. "We got stuck in a hole this morning. He got hurt when he lifted the wheel out."

"I've seen worse. The surgeons will splint it. We have the best surgeons in the army."

Downing gently replaced the blankets and remounted his horse.

"I take it you have come a long way."

"Yes, sir. From Ocracoke Island off North Carolina. About three hundred miles."

"Just the two of you? You and your father?"

"Yes, sir."

Downing straightened in his saddle. The sun shone straight down on his black horse and his black hair and his amazement.

"You will follow me," Downing ordered. "Move your wagon into the front of the line." He threw the reins into George's lap.

George hesitated, then asked, "How far? How far to Valley Forge?"

Downing laughed aloud, signaling with his right hand to the men he was leading. "Not far. About four hundred yards around the next bend. Not far at all. Follow me."

George stood up, as Erskin would have done, and drove the wagon to the front of the line. Greene's men fell in behind the wagon, and Downing moved everyone forward.

I have pulled my oar. George smiled to himself. I have pulled my oar at last.

From somewhere, not far at all, a rat-tat-tat bugle sounded the noon hour.

Author's Note

This story of the American Revolution is based on events that occurred during the winter of 1777-78.

Raids by parties of British sailors increased in frequency along the barrier islands. Citizens who would have remained Loyalist or neutral made a 180-degree turn against the crown.

With northern ports cut off by blockade, the supply situation at Valley Forge turned desperate after Christmas, 1777. January and February were abnormally cold. Death and desertion rates rose alarmingly. Even as the Continental Congress cut funds for supplies, severe weather shut down or delayed supply transport. The Valley Forge legend of endurance and courage was born during those two winter months.

In early February, General Washington received a letter from Governor Richard Caswell of North Carolina. Considerable quantities of salt and salted provisions, as well as blankets, shoes, and medicine had been secured at Portsmouth, on Ocracoke Inlet, and were being shipped by barge, canal boat, wagon, and horseback to Valley Forge. We have no authentic details as to how these shipments were made.

Regarding the lost colonists on Roanoke Island, many more Croatans—some 20 to 1—were lost or displaced than English settlers. In the early 1960s, a large area in north-western South Carolina became the site of a nuclear power plant. Several Indian villages were unearthed during construction. Among the thousands of artifacts, today preserved in a museum, are fragments of Croatan pottery and English porcelain.

The wind and sea shape and reshape the Outer Banks every day. Change is constant. Chicamacomico and Kinnakeet are now Rodanthe, Waves, and Salvo. Modern spellings on the map mark Erskin and George's journey through old waterways and contours.

Certain families—Midgett, Farrow, Fearing, Wahab, Etheridge, and Scarborough—continue to live on the Outer Banks. All characters in this story, however, are fictional.

SALLY EDWARDS